"What do you have that other women don't?"

Jay grasped her chin, tilting her face upward.

"Nothing," Danni replied, pushing him away. "I don't want to—get to you—as you call it, believe me!"

Jay moved even closer, studying her lazily. Finally he said softly, "You know what they say, Danni—yesterday's enemy, tomorrow's lover."

"Nonsense," Danni replied, ignoring his mocking smile. "I don't believe anybody ever said that. If they did, they didn't know what they were talking about."

Samantha Harvey had her first short story published when she was fifteen, followed by other short stories and articles for which she won awards for excellence. Her love of words, she believes, is inherited from her journalist father. Although she completed two successful television scripts, not until after her two sons had set out on their own did she find time to write romance novels. She and her husband live in a suburb of Melbourne, where, she claims, gardening gets rid of occasional writer's block— "I pull weeds and weave dreams at the same time." People and places fascinate her.

Books by Samantha Harvey

HARLEQUIN ROMANCE
2481—THE DRIFTWOOD BEACH
2522—THE DISTANCE MAN
2541—BOY WITH KITE
2764—AMARYLLIS DREAMING

Don't miss any of our special offers. Write to us at the following address for information on our newest releases.

Harlequin Reader Service
901 Fuhrmann Blvd., P.O. Box 1397, Buffalo, NY 14240
Canadian address: P.O. Box 603,
Fort Erie, Ont. L2A 5X3

Tomorrow's Lover

Samantha Harvey

Harlequin Books

TORONTO • NEW YORK • LONDON
AMSTERDAM • PARIS • SYDNEY • HAMBURG
STOCKHOLM • ATHENS • TOKYO • MILAN

Original hardcover edition published in 1987
by Mills & Boon Limited

ISBN 0-373-17013-0

Harlequin Romance first edition May 1988

CHAPTER ONE

DANNI PAIGE finished smoothing sunscreen over her long, slender legs, and Fiona leaned forward and took the plastic tube from her quietly. Danni sat perfectly still, her shoulders hunched, while Fiona smeared the cream over her back and shoulders until she was fully protected from the Queensland sun.

It was a near-perfect day, the sun gold, the sky piercing blue, and when she narrowed her eyes against the glitter of sun on water Danni could see the peaks of the twin hills on Jackson North's island showing in the distance. They made two blue triangles against the brighter blue of the sky, and Danni studied them quietly until Fiona finished and screwed the cap back on the tube.

Somebody said, 'You won't get much of a welcome out there. Jackson North is mighty fierce about his privacy. He'll probably throw you to the sharks,' and everybody laughed. Everybody, that was, except Danni and Fiona.

They were all sunbathing on the beach, Danni and her friends, their sailboards lying near the edge of the water; and when Danni announced that she planned riding her board over to Jackson North's island they all decided she must be out of her mind, and they said so.

Fiona put down the tube of sunscreen and studied Danni now with wide, troubled eyes.

'They say he keeps a shotgun in his cabin,' she murmured. 'Do you really have to go, Danni?'

'Yes, I do.' Danni managed to make it sound casual, she even succeeded in adding flippantly, 'If I'm not back by nightfall I give you permission to send Search and Rescue after me, but I don't expect to need any help.'

Fiona didn't look persuaded. She was Danni's best friend and she was really concerned. She thought, like all the others, that Danni wanted an interview for the local newspaper, but Danni had stronger reasons for visiting Jackson North. However, they were her Uncle Edwin's reasons and they were private, so she could not tell Fiona. Not yet, anyway.

Quickly, Danni folded her towel and put it beside Fiona's with the rest of her belongings and Fiona said with a worried frown, 'You met Jay North once, didn't you? I thought you didn't like him.'

'We didn't exactly meet,' Danni evaded carefully, 'he just happened to be at the television production studio in Brisbane one day when I went down to do a script. We weren't introduced.'

'But you didn't like him?' Fiona persisted.

'No, I didn't. Not much.'

That was an understatement. She hadn't liked the man at all and she was certain he hadn't liked her either. Even now she could raise a faint shiver at the memory of the look he had directed her way after their one and only encounter.

Fiona was looking at her oddly. It was very strange of Danni, her look said, to be setting out on that long ride across the water to try and find a man she didn't like. Everybody knew Jackson North wanted to be left alone. He was so protective about his privacy that people had stopped visiting his island long ago. They could look at him on their television screens, admiring the famous outback explorer in his documentaries, but he didn't want them visiting. Yet here was Danni, getting ready to go all that way——

Fiona sighed. 'I suppose you know what you're doing,' she allowed, although she didn't look at all convinced.

Danni stood up abruptly. If she didn't go now, while she had the will-power, she might not go at all, and that would be disastrous, not only for Uncle Edwin but for their whole family.

She was ready for the venture. Her long chestnut-brown hair was piled high on top of her head, tied with a white ribbon, the honey tan of her skin gleamed with suncream, and the pale blue lycra swimsuit clung to her figure like a second skin. Two young men carrying surf-boards along the beach whistled as she walked in front of them but Danni ignored them. She had other more important things on her mind.

The breeze was pleasant and steady with no capricious gusts, and any other time Danni knew she would have enjoyed the adventure. It was a challenge and Danni liked challenges. Today, however, she looked a lot more confident than she felt as she fitted the mast into its slot on the sailboard and stood for a few seconds sensing the wind direction before she pushed out on to the water and headed for the island.

Her body tanned and fit from the sea-sports that she loved, Danni had no fears about her ability to make the distance. Only today she had this sneaky feeling of apprehension, not because Fiona was unhappy and doubtful, but because she knew in her heart she could be chasing a lost cause. She could well meet with total rejection out on that island, and that would make her feel embarrassed or angry or both, and Danni didn't like negative feelings.

But nothing would have made Danni turn back, because in her mind she carried the haunting memory of Uncle Edwin's face, her mother and her brother Gregg standing beside him, with all the laughter wiped from their faces, all because of a letter written by Jackson North.

She could see them now, gathered in the office of the caravan park they operated, her uncle saying brokenly, 'He's got us. He wants all this land for sugar-cane, so we'll have to go,' before he crumpled the letter and dropped it on the counter.

Not if I can help it ... Danni hadn't spoken the words aloud but she murmured them now, with the wind blowing on her warm skin, her fingers curled around the boom, the colourful sail towering over her. You won't get away with this, Jackson North. Not if I can help it ...

As she left the shelter of land the wind strengthened and Danni became so involved in manoeuvring she scarcely noticed the passing of time and distance until she found herself approaching the southern headland of North's island.

She knew his cabin was hidden above this point behind the rocks but she wasn't expecting trouble with landing until she rounded the cliffs and a wide coral reef barred her passage. Its surface stretched above the water in the low tide as far as she could see, and Danni realised it offered an impassable barrier, even to a sailboard, while nobody in their right mind was going to walk barefoot over coral.

Slowly she tacked along the reef searching for an entrance. There had to be one because a slim white yacht rocked gently inside on the calmer water; but Danni was forced to travel almost the entire length of the beach before she found a break in the coral and headed for shore.

She carried her board on to the sand and stood breathing slowly and deeply, filling her lungs with calming fresh air. Then she raised her head and looked around her.

The long, white beach seemed to stretch for ever, and Danni gazed along it ruefully. For ever is a long way to walk when you know very well that at the other end someone waits with a definitely hostile reception.

Behind her on the mainland, the Capricorn coast looked far away, and Danni wished she were back there and that she had never heard of Jackson North.

It was really devious of the man, she decided crossly, to hide his cabin at the other end of the beach so that nobody could approach him unobserved. Her sail must have made a conspicuous splash of colour on the blue water—swirls of hot pink and turquoise dotted in black and white—and no doubt the owner of the island had plenty of warning that she was invading his privacy.

Danni straightened her shoulders and began to walk, and as she walked she reached up and untied the binding ribbon from her hair to let it blow dry in the breeze. For the first time she felt a little uneasy about approaching North so scantily clad, but it was difficult handling extra gear on a sailboard—anything she carried usually finished up as wet as herself—and she hadn't given it a thought because she certainly didn't expect to get this feeling of vulnerability as she made her way along the sand. Now, she would have welcomed something, a towel, a jacket, anything to drape around her so that she looked less naked, but of course it was too late.

She was half-way along the long stretch of sand when her skin began to tingle. There was no sign of life anywhere apart from occasional seabirds, but with a shock of recognition Danni knew instantly that somewhere ahead of her, behind the screening trees on the headland, Jackson North was already watching her approach.

She should have been prepared for this daunting and inexplicable reaction but perhaps she had blotted it out of her mind deliberately. Now as she walked along the sand Danni recalled the memory of her one and only encounter with Jackson North with uncomfortable clarity.

They had met, if you called it meeting, at Fennis-Gemini Television Productions in Brisbane, where Danni had recently been added to the list of scriptwriters on a daytime serial. This was her big chance and she had presented herself at the studios full of high hope.

Unfortunately she encountered traffic problems in the city and was running late. She remembered glancing anxiously at her wristwatch as she stepped out of the lift on the first floor of the studios, only to find her way barred by what looked like a crowd of excited schoolgirls. In the midst of the gathering a tall dark man stood casually signing autographs on notebooks, envelopes, pieces of paper, anything that was held out to him. She recognised him, of course, she had seen him often enough on television though he was larger than life offscreen.

He was Jackson North, Jay North to his loyal fans and viewers, and one of her brother Gregg's idols. Today there seemed an aura of excitement generated by the rapt, eager faces, or perhaps by the man himself. A powerful, dark-haired man with hawklike features, his tanned face hardened by two deep grooves running from nose to mouth, giving him an implacable look. He certainly didn't seem averse to the attention of his admirers. His eyes met Danni's, faintly amused, almost patronising, as she tried to weave her way through the crowd.

'If you don't mind——' she gasped, but nobody listened.

Clutching her notebook, Danni persevered until she stood almost beside him. His eyes were grey and very sharp, with a hint of mockery. They glinted at her as she tried to pass through the clamouring fans.

'I'm afraid you'll have to wait your turn,' he drawled.

'I'm not here for—I don't want——'

In her annoyance Danni imagined a suggestion of arrogance, even smugness, in the way he refused to step aside and let her pass through his clamouring fans. She made a desperate effort and pushed behind him, carrying with her the picture of his powerful figure dressed in light tan leather jacket worn casually loose over opennecked white shirt, silk probably, she guessed, and tight brown cord trousers held with a narrow belt with gold buckle and studs.

'Just what everybody's hero should look like,' Danni fumed cynically as she almost ran along the passageway, arriving at her story conference just in time.

Later that day when she went to the canteen for lunch somebody asked Danni, 'Did you see Jay North? Isn't he gorgeous?' and Danni had replied with unforgivable clarity, 'Yes, I saw him, but I wasn't impressed. Macho men don't turn me on,' and something in the faces around her told Danni instantly that she had blundered. Of course he must be there behind her, somewhere close enough to overhear that flippant comment.

She turned to meet the frosty grey eyes of the man she had last seen signing autographs. The bland halfsmile that touched his lips did not falter as his glance clashed with hers, so why did she receive the impression of a great and terrible anger directed towards her?

Danni recalled carrying her sandwiches and coffee to a corner table with two of the script editors, sitting with her back to where Jackson North settled himself in the centre of a respectful group, and all through the meal her skin had prickled, just as it was tingling now.

She had felt embarrassed at that time, although she tried hard not to show it; now, as she walked along that seemingly endless stretch of beach, Danni regretted her careless comment more than ever. The man had a right to be angry, she admitted it, and he had been very angry. So she had better face it: he wasn't going to be pleased to see her now, especially if he remembered that previous encounter.

Once, Danni imagined she caught on the headland in front of her a fleeting glitter of reflected sunlight on glass, and it came to her mind that perhaps the owner of the island was using binoculars to monitor her approach.

Uneasily she glanced behind her, seeing her footprints sharp and clear on the white sand. A hunter would have no trouble stalking her if he felt so inclined. She didn't like that thought. It seemed scary somehow, the way she felt vulnerable, as if she might be giving something of herself away in that long trail of clear footprints.

But she plodded on steadily, determinedly reminding herself she was here to defend her family, shoring up confidence by rehearsing silently in her head the things she planned to say to Jackson North when she found him.

'I want to know...' No, that sounded a little terse... 'I've come to ask, please, could you do a re-think about turning my family out of our caravan park just so you can grow a little more sugar-cane. Could you please not turn our lives upside down now that we've finally found somewhere to settle for the rest of our days...'

She walked steadily along the beach, head held high, as if the inward stirrings of doubt did not exist.

At the end of the sand she found a steep narrow track to the top of the headland. It didn't present any problems. Danni scaled it easily but as she hauled herself over the ledge at the top of the climb she found a fence barring her way with a gate baldly marked Private, and this time she hesitated.

Once she pushed open that small white gate she would be trespassing. If North had a gun then maybe he also kept a dog, or dogs, to keep intruders away.

Steeling herself, Danni pushed.

The gate swung easily on its hinges and she waited, listening for sounds among the trees, hearing nothing but the rustling palms. If North had a pack of hounds to guard him they were apparently busy elsewhere, and Danni let out her breath in a sigh of relief. She hadn't realised how uneasy she was until this moment.

The path led across a clearing surrounded by rock terraces smothered in colourful vines, and Danni found herself facing a small cabin. It looked like only three or four rooms with a veranda roofed in clear green plastic, and Danni walked up three steps, crossed the veranda and rapped on the door.

There was no response. Of course not. If the occupier had watched her approaching he wasn't going to admit her now. Visitors were not welcome here. The whole place might have been deserted but Danni knew it wasn't. Her skin told her. It still tingled.

She rapped again on the door, this time louder, and the harsh sound seemed an invasion of the calm around her, making her feel guilty; but when nothing happened she stepped determinedly closer and hammered on the door with both hands.

When it jerked open Danni nearly plummeted inside. She saved herself by grasping the door-handle, and the man facing her gave one raking look before he rasped, 'For heaven's sake, don't bang the door down! I know you're here. The whole of Australia probably knows you're here by now. What the devil do you want?'

Danni steadied herself. 'You are Jackson North of Jannorth Enterprises?'

'Do you really have to ask?' His lips tightened in grim irony. 'Anyway, what's it to you?'

He stood barring her way, a slight frown creasing his wide tanned forehead, gazing down at her with undisguised hostility, and Danni steadied herself again. This was no time to become intimidated. She wasn't going to get a welcome here, so it was just as well she hadn't expected one.

Resolutely doing her best to look casual-cool, she studied her adversary warily. No wonder people found him daunting. He must be one of the fittest men she had ever seen, and she saw plenty of them on the beaches. But this man had something extra. It wasn't only size and strength, it had something to do with the way he held himself, aloof and challenging, crackling with confidence.

Darn the man! He must be surely the most arrogant person Danni had ever encountered.

Today the strong, tanned body was clad only in black briefs and an unbuttoned cotton shirt, yellow and faded, revealing most of a muscled torso. The dark hair, massed crisp curls over his forehead but dipping to the back of his neck in tumbled clusters, gave him a raffish air. Positively piratical, was Danni's first reaction, and her second that he looked every inch a predator, and a dangerous one at that. He also appeared extremely annoyed.

'I don't recall issuing any invitations. I hope you're not expecting to be invited inside.'

Danni managed to meet his ironic gaze but it took all her will-power. 'I was hoping you would talk to me.'

'Is that so? Perhaps you'd like to tell me why I should spend my valuable time talking to you?'

He stood in the doorway, deliberately inspecting Danni's figure, his glance travelling insolently over the scanty bathing suit, travelling over every inch of golden skin; he didn't miss a curve or a plane, and to Danni's dismay the inspection was like the scan from a powerful machine. It shook her control but she managed to stand there without flinching. If her skin had tingled before, sensation was rampant now.

The cool appraisal continued over suntanned legs, even noting the square-cut toenails polished faintest pink yet obviously trimmed for action. Then his glance travelled deliberately back to Danni's face. Glacial grey eyes flicked her coldly, then suddenly narrowed.

'How much?'

Danni glared at him truculently. 'What do you mean, how much? Are you insinuating——?'

'Don't tell me you aren't here to offer your charms? They're certainly on display, aren't they?'

Danni put ice into her voice. 'I hope you're not suggesting what I think you are.'

He eyed her coolly. 'Yes, I am,' he replied with awful calm. 'What do you expect, throwing yourself on my doorstep practically naked?'

The gibe in his taunting voice sent a surge of resentment through Danni that bolstered her courage miraculously.

'There are thousands of girls over there,' she waved a hand towards the mainland beach, 'dressed exactly like me or wearing even less. Some of them in bikinis.'

'Yes,' he agreed smoothly, 'but they aren't on my doorstep.'

'And I'm not on your doorstep for that purpose.'

The man's lips curved derisively. 'Pity,' he drawled. 'What I can see—and I guess that's most of it—looks reasonably inviting. I'm sure we could have whiled away an hour or two quite pleasantly.'

Danni's eyes flashed fire. 'You must read the wrong kind of books or you get your foul ideas in some strange places,' she snapped. 'Let's get this straight. I didn't come here to go to bed with you. I came to try and have a reasonable conversation. I hope that's not too much to ask.'

He studied her for a moment silently, then to Danni's surprise stood suddenly aside, silently motioning her to walk ahead of him. He waved her across a large living-room, before opening another door, and Danni found herself in a small study with a large flat-topped desk holding a typewriter, with scattered files and papers around it. There were shelves along the side walls, piled with more folders and books.

Jackson North walked around the desk and seated himself in the chair, and Danni wondered with fleeting suspicion whether he chose that position purposely to give himself the advantage: he the interrogator, she the intruder...

Then he pointed to a chair, but she did not sit down, only stood facing him quietly, and he watched her inscrutably for a moment before he said, 'All right, you have three minutes. Tell me what you want and make it fast. What's your subject?'

Impulsively Danni offered, 'I thought we might have a discussion about dirty tricks.'

His lips twitched faintly. 'If that's your idea of a reasonable conversation, you could do with a few lessons in diplomacy.'

'All right, I'll tell you. It's about the sugar-cane plantation you are planning to buy,' she began, and he snapped to instant attention.

'Have bought,' he amended sharply. 'And what's that to do with you?'

His rudeness irritated Danni. He was making her feel defensive, and she didn't like it.

'I want to know why you are hounding my family and I've come to tell you to stop it.'

She sounded a lot more confident than she felt. There was something incredibly daunting in the way he looked at her, those steely grey eyes piercing, fingers clenched around a pen he had picked up, as if he wished it were a missile and his desk a launching pad. He didn't like being interrupted at his work, that was for sure. Those eyes were frosty and impatient, as well as unfriendly.

He drawled silkily, 'Just who is this family I'm supposed to be—ah—hounding?' and his lips tightened as he put down the pen and pushed the papers away from his typewriter.

Danni summoned her courage. She moistened her lips. 'We—my family—we run the caravan park on part of the land. There was an understanding between my uncle and the previous owners of the property that we could use it.'

'Your uncle!' That really jerked him to attention. He leaned forward in his chair as if he were tensed, ready for action. 'Are you telling me Edwin Paige is your uncle?'

'Yes, I am.'

He gave one short hard laugh that had no amusement in it at all. 'Does that mean you could be Ryan Paige's daughter?' He asked the question incredulously, as if this were something he couldn't believe, and when she nodded his lips curved into an unmistakable sneer. 'Well, I'll be damned!'

There seemed some sort of innuendo there and Danni reacted fiercely. 'You probably will be.' She met his bitter glance with as much confidence as she could summon up, before she added defiantly, 'My name is Danielle Paige. I'm Ryan Paige's daughter and proud of it.'

'Ryan Paige's daughter.' His face darkened. 'And you have the effrontery to talk to me about dirty tricks! That's a laugh. Your old man was the dirtiest trickster of them all.'

Danni searched his face for some kind of mockery, some suggestion that he might be baiting her, but something in that grim expression told her Jackson North was very, very angry and meant every word he said. The whole room vibrated with his anger.

Danni sank down slowly on to the edge of the chair he had indicated a few minutes ago, still watching his expression, until her composure returned and she announced clearly,

'My father never played a dirty trick in his life. He's dead now, but I know he wasn't that kind of man.'

Some of the harshness faded from North's features, although when he spoke there was still ice in his voice.

'Then perhaps you had better take a good hard look at your dear uncle, because one of the Paige brothers, if not both, were responsible for——' he turned away from the desk for a silent moment and when he turned back again his face was enigmatic '—for something I'd rather not talk about, but believe me it was dirty.'

Danni stammered, 'My uncle says you bought our land on purpose, to make it hard for us and turn us out. He says you're hounding him.'

'I'd need to have a reason, wouldn't I? Did he mention that?'

'No.' Uncle Edwin had muttered something about there being 'a streak of madness in the North family', adding that 'Jay North's father was quite batty, of course,' but Danni wasn't going to repeat that.

She hadn't planned for the discussion to go in this direction. For her mother's sake—for all their sakes—she had to keep a rein on her temper, although she would have liked to lash back at the man who sat there with contempt in his eyes, his whole expression so aloof and challenging.

'I'm sorry.' She hated the stiffness in her own apology, and she knew the man at the desk picked it up too. She added placatingly, 'I came here to appeal to your better nature,' and to her utter amazement he tilted back his head and laughed.

'Surely you could come up with something more original than that. A girl with your imagination and flair should be able to produce something a little less obvious. I'm sure there's a fertile imagination lurking behind those innocent green eyes.' He was goading her, a definite challenge in the eyes that glinted at her across the desk.

Danni determined not to let her own gaze falter before the formidable challenge. She faced him defiantly, eyes as wide and steady as she could make them, and slowly the atmosphere in the study underwent a subtle change. The man was still trying to intimidate her, Danni was sure of it, but a strange expression flickered behind the icy grey eyes and he seemed to tense and freeze.

It was hard to define what triggered the change; one instant they were two hostile strangers, assessing each other, neither liking what they saw and felt. The next, they seemed to become electrically aware of each other, and a vibrancy in the room seemed to draw the walls closer as if the air were suddenly hard to breathe. Danni heard the pounding of her own heartbeats.

Jackson North pushed back his chair and stood up. Danni licked dry lips. She didn't like the way he was looking at her.

Then abruptly he turned and strode into the next room, coming back with a white shirt over his arm.

'Here.' He tossed the garment to Danni. 'For heaven's sake cover yourself,' he ordered tersely, 'before I treat you exactly as you deserve to be treated.'

It looked as if she had lost control of this interview, if she had ever had it. Obediently, Danni shook out the shirt, stood up, pushed her arms into the sleeves and draped the garment around her. With fingers unaccountably clumsy she knotted the fronts at her waist, and then stood there, staring at her adversary. North raised his eyebrows, while a fleeting smile tilted the corners of the wide mouth.

'Not exactly my style,' he commented drily. 'I wear it differently. But at least the rest of the discussion won't be so distracting. Sit down.'

Danni sat obediently. Instinct told her they had just experienced a dangerous moment, and she wasn't going to ask for trouble by antagonising this unpredictable man.

'Now,' he challenged her, 'let's see if we can continue our discussion. What were you saying?'

Danni drew another deep breath. 'I was saying, surely you couldn't be so destructive——' that didn't sound tactful and she slanted a hasty look in his direction but he wasn't reacting '—surely you can't intend putting a hard-working family out of business just to grow more sugar-cane, when you know perfectly well——'

'I don't know anything perfectly well.' The leniency was gone from his expression now. Danni wasn't reaching him and she knew it. She stared at him helplessly.

'You aren't willing to listen to reason?'

'It isn't reason you're offering me. It's sentiment. How can I be responsible for putting somebody out of business if he didn't have the common sense to make sure it was safe to lay out a caravan park on part of somebody else's sugar-farm?'

'He was promised——'

'Rubbish. Would you coast along on the strength of someone's vague promise?'

No, she wouldn't, but her uncle would. Edwin Paige had a childlike faith in the promises of others. It had been his undoing more than once.

Danni tried again. 'Don't you feel obliged to honour an agreement?'

He sounded almost bored. 'I've seen no agreement. I don't feel the slightest compulsion to honour an agreement that might never have existed.'

He leaned back in his chair, his eyes taunting her, and Danni challenged him. 'Are you saying I'm a liar?'

'You allege there was an agreement. Let's see you prove it. Until then I'm afraid there's nothing I can do.'

Danni persisted. 'My uncle spent all his money, we all have, every cent we owned, setting up this caravan park. Uncle Ed wouldn't have done that without some assurance.'

'So he'll have to move his equipment elsewhere.' North sounded indifferent.

'No, he can't. You know that. What about the permanent installations, showers and toilets, the laundry, the shop and office building? You know very well he can't uproot everything and move to another locality.'

'Shouldn't he have thought of that before? Most people—most sensible people—cover themselves with a written contract before going haywire with that kind of expenditure. Your uncle doesn't sound a very capable businessman.'

'My uncle trusts people. The previous owners promised they wouldn't sell the land and now they have.' Her eyes flashed. 'How did you persuade them, I wonder?'

Jackson North actually laughed again, a grim laugh maybe, but it held a dash of wry humour.

'Your uncle may be a deplorable businessman but you're an even worse intermediary. You are here to ask favours, I presume, but you've done nothing but insult me since you belted on my front door.'

'You aren't going to listen to me, anyway.' Defeat made a bitter taste in Danni's mouth. She stood up furiously. 'You'd better have your shirt back. I'll find some other way——'

'Wait.' Danni had begun untying the shirt but the man at the desk motioned her impatiently back to the chair. He picked up the pen, tapping restlessly on the papers beside him. 'Maybe there's another way right here. We could strike a bargain.'

'What kind of bargain?' Danni eyed him suspiciously, and the grim smile appeared again.

'You are in no position to argue about what kind of bargain, are you? It just so happens I find myself in a slight predicament at the moment. What were you doing at the television studios?'

So he did remember. Danni's heart sank. She could have done without that but she explained as steadily as she could, 'I had a contract to write a script. I was reporting for a story conference.'

'Scriptwriter, are you?' He gave her the same impersonal once-over he might have given any strange creature who turned up on his doorstep. Then he added, 'My regular assistant went overseas after we thought we'd finished the last documentary. I hired a substitute but he told me yesterday he has to go home to Adelaide in South Australia, so that leaves me in a bit of a hole. How are you on layout, timing, that sort of thing?'

'I can cope.' She wasn't going to tell him she was a novice and that was her first script. Besides, she didn't like him. Danni steeled herself to meet his probing glance with confidence. He couldn't have sounded more remote.

'If you help me out I might consider co-operating with your family about the caravan park. Can you type?'

Danni nodded. He vacated his chair, pushed it back from the desk. 'Show me.'

Typing was one of Danni's strengths. She settled herself in the chair, rolled a sheet of paper into the machine and rattled off several lines. Thank heavens it was a similar typewriter to the one Uncle Edwin kept in the office at the caravan park. Mercifully she made no mistakes.

She pulled the paper from the machine and thrust it towards him. He read it swiftly, nodded, put it down on the desk.

'All right. Can you be ready to start tomorrow?'

'Yes. My script is finished.'

'OK, you work for me for the next two or three weeks, however long it takes, and I'll allow your family the use of the land they now occupy for another three to five years. Is it a deal?'

Danni nodded agreement.

'I take it you can handle outback travel?'

'Outback travel!' Danni stared at him aghast. 'Look, I said I'll do some work for you. I meant here or on the mainland.'

'I have to take a second look at some of the ground covered in my last documentary.'

'No.'

'In that case,' he settled back in his own chair, pulling the typewriter towards him, 'we'll consider the matter closed.' The eyes that met her glance briefly across the paper-strewn desk were ice-hard. 'End of interview.'

That was an ultimatum.

'You aren't even willing to discuss my working here?' Of course he wasn't. Danni gazed at him speculatively across the desk. He ignored her, as if waiting for her to turn on her heel and leave, and she couldn't do it. Not with the recollection of Uncle Edwin's anguished face as she had seen it this morning.

Danni stood up, taking off his shirt, shaking herself free. She folded the garment with shaking fingers and tossed it over the back of the chair.

'I—I'll have to let you know. I'll talk it over with my family.'

He glanced up briefly, the flicker in his eyes looking suspiciously like ironic amusement. 'Having second thoughts?'

'I suppose I'll have to, if that's the only way you'll help us.'

'It is, believe me.' The dark man's voice hardened as if he had become suddenly more impatient. He added brusquely, 'I'll be over on the mainland early tomorrow morning. I've an office down south in Rockhampton. Write down your phone number on that piece of paper and I'll call the caravan park, so you can let me know finally if you're available. You understand—no deal, no caravan park. I shall expect you to stick to your part of the bargain and do what's required, when it's required.'

'In a professional capacity,' Danni found herself interjecting before she could censor her wayward tongue.

He picked up her thoughts instantly, surprising her with a fleeting grin that momentarily transformed the hard features, but quickly disappeared.

'Don't worry. Bedroom duties are out. You may find yourself involved in the odd spot of cooking or washing.' He went on, 'We'll be using separate small tents most of the time, but in any case you need not fear for your maidenly modesty, if any.' Once again his glance flicked over her scanty covering. 'I can get what I want in that line without hassles. I don't have to beg.'

He watched an indignant Danni scribble her telephone number on the paper. 'You can drive?'

'Yes, I have my licence.'

'Good. And bring your stopwatch if you have one. I may need you to handle some of the timing.'

Face expressionless, he reached out and picked up the paper with her telephone number, putting it beside his typewriter. It was after midday but he didn't ask if Danni wanted lunch or even a cup of tea. He simply said, 'I take it you can get back to shore the way you came. I'll be in touch in the morning. Have your answer ready. I don't have time to hang around.'

It was a dismissal, and Danni fumed as she let herself out, descended the cliff path and set out on the long walk back to her sailboard.

Her skin told her Jackson North had not bothered to watch her go. She experienced none of the electric awareness, none of the sensual disturbance that happened whenever she felt his eyes on her. And for that, she assured herself vehemently, she was grateful.

Yet as she launched her board on to the water, measuring with keen eyes the distance from island to shore, she felt a little lost, a little lonely, as if her confidence had taken a beating and she could have done with some moral support.

She let the sail feather loosely in the breeze before she braced herself, using the strength of her body to control the coloured sail as it tautened and filled with wind, ready to take her away from Jackson North and his island.

All the way home her mind worked furiously. Nothing, she decided fiercely, would persuade her to go tripping into the outback with a man like Jackson North. She wouldn't trust him an inch. He was a predator, a dangerous man, perhaps even an immoral one. She told herself uneasily there had to be something suspicious in the ease with which he had produced the job he wanted her to do. You can't trust the Norths, her uncle had said this morning. Maybe he knew something she didn't.

She dug deep in her mind, searching for alternatives. There had to be some other way to solve their problem. Maybe she would arrive home and find her uncle had already worked something out . . . maybe.

CHAPTER TWO

IT WAS late afternoon when Danni reached the golden beach north of Rockhampton, on the Capricorn coast of Queensland, that was now home to her.

All her friends had left the beach. She stowed her sailboard in the boatshed where Fiona had left her other belongings, and a few minutes later as she opened the door of her small red sports car to drive to the caravan park, Danni could not resist a backward glance to where the peaks of Jay North's island showed faintly. 'Like shark fins against the sky,' she decided crossly. 'Very appropriate.'

The road wound along the riverside for almost a mile, and as she approached the frangipani trees on the grass outside the entrance to the caravan park, Danni glimpsed her uncle walking along the driveway. He moved slowly, shoulders hunched in the body language of weariness and despair, and Danni guessed instantly that he had not found any way out of their difficulty.

By the time she turned into the park he had disappeared into the white wooden building beside the entrance that housed the reception counter and office and a small store. She parked her car between the two caravans her family used as living-quarters, and when she walked into the store one look at the faces of the three people standing there told her nobody had come up with any miracles while she was away.

It was quiet in the park, most of the residents still away fishing in the river or relaxing on the ocean beaches, so there was no one except Danni, her mother and brother Gregg to hear the despair in Edwin Paige's voice.

He looked up defensively as Danni came in. 'I've been busy all day, don't think I haven't. It's all legal, what this fellow North says in his letter. He's purchased the whole property and he wants the lot for growing sugarcane, so he won't talk to me or listen to reason. His lawyer just laughed when I asked for a discussion. Says he's too busy. So,' Edwin's soft round face quivered, 'it's goodbye caravan park.'

'Surely he'll give us back the money we've spent?' Gregg, nineteen years old, should have been out watering the gardens but he hovered around hopefully. His uncle shook his head.

'No. We have three months to get out, and that's it.' Edwin Paige spread his hands helplessly. 'Where would we find another piece of land around here the size of this one? I got this deal from the Jensens because we were mates. At least, I thought we were.'

Danni asked desperately, 'Didn't you get anything in writing? Not anything at all?' and her uncle moved uncomfortably, his usually placid face tight with anxiety.

'I didn't need anything on paper,' he defended himself. 'Promises are promises between friends.' He looked anxiously at Danni's mother and Gregg. 'I'm not very good at business——'

No, he wasn't. They had survived several disasters over the years since her father's death, but this caravan park on the Capricorn coast had flourished since he put the first permanent vans in place three years ago and marked out other sites for travellers. They had all believed their luck had changed at last. Then along came Jackson North...

Edwin Paige looked at Danni, a furrow between his brows. 'How was I to know the land would be sold? I took a gamble.'

The story of his life, Danni thought wryly. Always taking gambles, never understanding when they didn't come off. Not that you could blame him.

Danni looked affectionately at her uncle's face, almost childlike in its round and rosy smoothness under the white hair.

He mumbled, 'Vindictive, that's what it is, just plain vindictive. He's done it on purpose, after all these years,' and Danni's heart went cold. He wasn't talking about the Jensens surely, he must mean Jackson North, and Danni asked steadily, 'Did something happen between you and the North family, Uncle Ed? What was it?'

Her uncle shrugged but he didn't look at her.

'Who knows? I can't remember details. It was all so long ago. You and Gregg were only children, living in Adelaide with your mother.'

He would have left it at that but Gregg, sensing a story, urged him, 'Go on, tell us,' and Edwin glanced at their expectant faces before he continued uneasily, 'It happened while we were digging for opals in central Australia, your father, Gardiner North, and myself. Going to make our fortunes, we were.'

'Was that Jackson North's father?'

'Yes. Very optimistic we were, you know how young fellows are. Anyway, we had a—a little business mix-up because the only opal we found turned out to be practically worthless. North reckoned it should have been worth more than we got. He was very unreasonable about it. Carried on like a lunatic, reckoning it was our fault we didn't make a fortune or some rubbish like that. Bit of insanity in the family, if you ask me. Now it looks as if we'll all have to pay for something that happened years ago.'

Lilyan Paige spoke for the first time, directly to Edwin. 'You believe Jackson North planned this deliberately, as some kind of foolish revenge?' and her brother-in-law disclaimed hastily, 'Who knows? Maybe it's pure co-incidence Gardiner North's son should buy this land.' But he sounded doubtful. His voice lingered on the word 'maybe', as if he couldn't accept it.

Danni moved to the window, blinking back tears as she stared at the caravans glinting in the afternoon sunshine. Permanent vans lined the perimeter of the park, with sites for overnighters and casual travellers arranged in a central block bounded by a gravel driveway.

Sugar-cane bordered the park on three sides. There were no fences, and when the burning of the cane was in progress the cane toads thronged the grassy spaces of the park and smoke hung low; but the cane was growing tall now, plumes waving in the sun, and Danni thought it beautiful.

At the rear of the park a shallow lagoon glistened, birds floated on the water or probed the grassy banks for food, and Danni noticed through the tears gathering in her eyes that Rose and Emily Barton were feeding the ibis again.

The plump white birds, with black tails and sickle beaks, clustered outside the permanent van feeding on proffered scraps, and Danni thought, How could anybody want to destroy all this? How dare they?

She came out of her musing to hear her brother saying, 'There goes another hero! I always thought Jay North was the greatest. Guess I just can't pick 'em.'

Lilyan Paige sat quite still, light from the window touching her face, and something Danni saw there startled her. The bright light revealed her delicate skin fretted with a network of fine lines, her lips pale, hands lying so unnaturally still, almost lifeless on her lap; and Danni saw this latest disaster had shaken her mother more than the others. She was looking at a woman who had suffered too many setbacks.

Since her husband's death Lilyan Paige had become introspective. Now Danni saw with a pang that her mother was close to being defeated, and her heart ached.

She walked from the window before she said steadily, 'I went to see Jackson North today, and I made a deal with him. He needs an assistant because he has some work he wants done in a hurry, and if I do it for him he'll give us at least another few years to sort ourselves out.'

'I told you something would turn up!'

The instant change from defeat to triumph in her uncle was frightening. He looked immediately as if all his problems had been solved, and he shrugged them off so fast that when a motorist slowed, read the sign over the gate and towed his van outside the office, Edwin picked up the white peaked cap he always wore out of doors, arranged it carefully over his abundant white hair, and walked outside jauntily.

Danni saw that as he directed the driver to a camping-site he was actually beaming as if he hadn't a care in the world.

He hadn't stopped to ask how and where she met Jackson North, or what work had to be done, and Danni knew he didn't intend to. She stared after her uncle numbly and her mother said softly, 'Danni, you aren't planning to do anything foolish, are you?'

She was studying her daughter's pensive face, and her eyes were troubled.

Danni had forgotten those flashes of perception her mother often had. They were working well today, because Danni knew now that when North rang tomorrow morning she would have to tell him she would be ready to travel with him, and that was the most difficult decision she had ever had to make in all her twenty-two years.

She knew she must tell Lilyan now, straight away, because if she hesitated too long about it she could be dissuaded, and that would be the end of everything.

She said as casually as she could, 'Don't worry, Mums. I'm not planning anything I can't handle. I'll have to do some outback travelling with the man. He needs some extra film and information to finish off his latest documentary, and when that's done he's agreed not to take over the park until we're ready, or maybe not at all.'

Gregg whistled, a soft low whistle under his breath, but Danni got the message. 'I'm not sleeping with him,' she snapped.

'I should hope not!' Lilyan Paige sounded horrified, and Danni's young brother said morosely,

'Just goes to show you can't judge people from a television screen. I always wanted to be like him. Now I'll punch his nose if he gets fresh, and you can tell him so.' But his young voice sounded disillusioned.

Lilyan watched her daughter carefully. 'Are you really sure you know what you're doing, Danni?'

'Of course. I'm quite certain.' Danni offered her mother a quick smile. It was meant to be totally reassuring but Lilyan kept looking at her with those faintly questioning eyes, so Danni moved quickly across the room and picked up the typewritten letter her uncle had left carelessly on the counter.

She pushed it quickly into the bottom drawer behind the counter and pushed the drawer in sharply before she turned the key and locked it away, out of sight. Then she hung the key in the usual place, hidden above the cabinet where her uncle kept his records.

'Don't worry, Mums.' She dropped a kiss on her mother's still head. 'I'll do this work for our new landlord and maybe things will come right for Uncle Ed and all of us this time.' She even managed a teasing chuckle. 'Poor old dear. He can't be wrong all the time.

Perhaps this time he's on a winner. Anyway, what are setbacks for, except to be overcome?'

Danni tried to say the words lightly, with confidence, but as she moved to walk outside, passing her brother near the doorway, he murmured softly so that her mother could not hear,

'I wouldn't go if I were you, sister dear. Not gadding off into the wilds with a man like Jackson North.'

'You look after the shop. I've things to do,' Danni ordered him sharply.

He pulled a face at her. 'Have you told Derek yet? He won't like it, you know.'

As if she didn't have any troubles to deal with, here was another she had overlooked in her confusion. Derek wouldn't like it at all. Not that he had a great deal of say in her life as yet, but he was pleasant company, and this could be the end of a happy relationship, if he should read into the arrangement things that were not there.

Danni walked out into the sunny afternoon, un-usually thoughtful. She was supposed to be going to a dinner-dance with Derek tonight. She flexed her tired muscles ruefully. The last thing she fancied at the moment was a night out. Tomorrow morning Jackson North would telephone, and she must be ready for him.

She wasn't foolish enough to imagine it would be easy, travelling with a demanding, probably unreasonable man who would certainly expect some hard work in return for favours granted. But Danni straightened her shoulders as she opened the door of the caravan she shared with her mother. She ought to be able to handle it. It was after all just a difficult job that might have its compensations in the knowledge she would absorb as she worked.

She would have to get busy sorting out clothing to pack, but first there was the problem of her date with

Derek. Maybe she would be able to talk herself out of it.

Fiona's brother Derek was a local artist who owned a souvenir shop and art gallery along the riverside, where a small collection of shops lured tourists from the highway. Danni helped with the making of souvenirs, keeping up a supply of hand-painted T-shirts and tops. Some she decorated with flowers, kangaroos or koala bears, others with saucy slogans. It was a sideline she enjoyed, and occasionally she helped out with sales as well if the caravan park wasn't busy and she did not have a writing assignment.

Danni knew that Fiona was secretly expecting that some day she would have Danni not only as friend, but as her brother's wife. She wasn't exactly matchmaking, but the friendship between Danni and Derek was developing very nicely, thank you, and Fiona was obviously delighted.

Derek's mother was not quite so encouraging. A tall, determined woman with short-cropped grey hair and probing blue eyes, she regarded her son as a valuable prize and intended to make difficulties for anybody she considered unworthy of him.

She wasn't sure about Danni, she had already made that clear on several occasions. Danni was a little too adventurous, a little too independent; and her voice was as icy as her eyes about half an hour later as she watched Danni turned her red car into the parking-space outside the gallery and jump out to greet Fiona.

'She's here.' Her son did not answer.

Danni had changed into a green skirt with a loose body shirt over it, and Derek's mother obviously didn't care for the raffish green crab waving a spray of Cooktown orchids that Danni had painted across the front. Her eyebrows lifted delicately at the large bone earrings dangling from Danni's ears.

Danni had dressed that way on purpose, choosing something light-hearted to lift her spirits, but one look at Derek's mother's face told her it wasn't such a good idea. She was meeting with a very critical reception.

Fiona flung herself at Danni in enthusiastic relief. 'Thank goodness you're back!' She hugged Danni tightly then waved a hand towards the gallery.

'I told them where you went——' she turned apologetically to her friend '—I hope you don't mind, Danni—I was so worried——'

'Of course I don't mind. Why should I?'

Danni assumed a light-heartedness she did not feel as she walked past the front window adorned with sea relics and entered the gallery where Derek had become suddenly engrossed in the new mural he had just put up on the wall. He must have heard her come in talking to Fiona but he did not look around. His mother said tersely, 'Derek, here's Danni,' and he mumbled sulkily, 'What's this about you sailboarding out to Jackson North's island?'

'That's right. I went out this morning.'

Still Derek did not look around from the mural. 'Bit idiotic, wasn't it?'

'Of course not. I enjoyed it.'

It was difficult to sound airy and casual with Derek's mother scrutinising her out of those disapproving eyes, but Danni managed it.

Derek was now giving her his attention. 'You could have got into trouble. Whatever possessed you?'

'I had to see Jackson North. It was important.'

'Oh.' He stared at her suspiciously. 'Well, I hope you haven't forgotten about tonight.'

No, she hadn't forgotten she was supposed to be going out with him tonight but she had hoped to excuse herself. She would need a sharp brain and a clear head tomorrow.

She glanced doubtfully from Derek to his watching mother.

'No. I haven't forgotten.'

There was a party of them going dining and dancing at a charity affair Derek considered important. He wanted to be seen there. Danni found herself wishing desperately that Derek's mother would leave and let her explain to Derek and Fiona about her plans; but the older woman stood firm as the furniture. She scented something in the air and she wasn't going to miss any of it.

Danni moved closer to the mural Derek had been studying. 'It's beautiful.' She touched it reverently. 'I wish I could afford one.' And then, because it seemed they were all waiting, she announced clearly, 'I've promised to do some work for Mr—for Jackson North. It means I'll have to join him on an outback trip. It'll be a wonderful experience. I expect I'll learn a lot that will help with my writing.'

She was talking too much and too fast but the thunderstruck silence was intimidating and Fiona's eyes had widened in horror. Then she giggled uncomfortably.

'But I thought you didn't——'

'Didn't like Jackson North,' Danni filled in for her quickly. 'You don't have to like a man to work for him. I need every bit of experience I can get, and I might never get a chance like this again.' That sounded pretty lame, even to Danni, and she added hurriedly, feeling devious, 'Besides, he was in an awkward position. He couldn't get anybody——'

'Of course,' Fiona agreed too quickly, trying to ignore the disapproval on her brother's face.

Derek's mother interrupted firmly, 'How well do you know this man?' and Danni confessed,

'Not very.'

The atmosphere was growing unpleasant. Derek didn't get angry very often but he was showing clear signs of annoyance now, and when he repeated, 'About tonight ' looking at Danni belligerently, Danni hesitated. If they were going to fight, she didn't want it to be in front of Derek's mother.

She ventured, 'I thought perhaps Fiona might——' and Fiona said quickly, 'I'm going with Jimmy, don't you remember? That makes twelve of us at the table, the exact number Derek wanted.'

'All right, but I might have to leave early.' Danni capitulated, and Derek looked faintly mollified.

He said pointedly, 'Wear that scarlet dress, will you, the one I like. I want you to look spectacular. I'll pick you up about half past seven.'

Derek would not look spectacular himself, but he was reasonably handsome and he would look pleasant and cool and charming, and he would be nice to all the people who mattered.

He liked all the publicity he could get, it was good for the gallery. That was probably why he wished her to wear the scarlet dress, because he thought it might attract the cameras.

As she drove home to the park Danni found herself wondering whether that might be why Derek liked to take her out, because she could look spectacular when he asked her to. She honestly regretted her lack of enthusiasm about their date tonight. She really liked being with Derek. He was good company and their shared interests made the time they spent together pass easily and agreeably.

Yet as she parked her car and walked into the caravan ready to start packing, she could have done without the memory of the petulance in Derek's expression.

She found her suitcase and a small canvas carry-all and began sorting out tops and shorts and skirts. Nothing attractive, she warned herself, nothing sexy that might activate the wrong kind of ideas in a stranger's unpredictable imagination. She almost giggled then, recalling Gregg's reaction and her own sharp 'I'm not sleeping with the man', and the vaguest frisson of doubt, a suspicion of uncomfortable foreboding, stirred in her mind.

Swiftly she smothered her uneasiness. What was it he had said? 'I can get what I want without hassles...' And she had made her position clear, so she should have nothing to worry about.

She collected a couple of spare typewriter ribbons, the stopwatch, notebooks and pens. No doubt North would have his own tape recorder if one was required.

She wondered about taking her own camera but decided she had better travel light. After all, she would be there to work. If only she could put away from her memory the sound of Gregg's voice: 'I wouldn't go if I were you, sister dear.' If only she could stifle her doubts, she might even manage to look forward to the journey.

An early night would have been a great help but it wasn't to be. The long sailboard rides had taken their toll, and later as she pulled the long scarlet dress over her shoulders and smoothed it over her hips Danni knew her face looked paler than usual.

She gathered every gold chain necklace she owned and hung them around her neck in a riot of sparkling. Then she added glittering golden earrings, even a couple of dress-rings she rarely wore. Derek wanted her to attract attention tonight, and she would do her best for him.

She hesitated over splashing gold sparkles on to her hair, then compromised by sprinkling just the merest glitter. A little overdone perhaps, but Derek wanted impact and he would get it.

As a freelance writer Danni occasionally wrote articles for the local newspapers. The reporter and photographer on duty that night hailed her cheerfully as they moved among tables.

'Feel free to take any pictures you want,' Derek urged
them and they obliged. The young cameraman was arranging Danni under a wall-lamp that reflected the glitter
in her hair when she suddenly tuned in to disharmony.
Someone was watching her, not pleasantly.

Danni turned her head and found two people in a
dimly lit alcove on the other side of the hall. The girl
was blonde, her features blurred by the play of light and
shadows, but Jay North was unmistakable. Those grim
features, sardonic disapproval in every line, watched
cynically as Danni posed for the photographer, Derek
hovering solicitously close, an arm around her shoulders.

No doubt she looked as if she were lapping up the
attention, and perversely Danni produced her most provocative smile as the camera clicked.

Jackson North could think what he liked. He should
be out there on his island, not sitting across the room
at that half-hidden table making her feel embarrassed.

She turned her back on him and his shadowy companion, concentrating fiercely on Derek. He was delighted at her fervent attention and Danni felt guilty.
Whatever was the matter with her?

Derek danced attention on her for the rest of the
evening. Why shouldn't he? Everything had gone well,
photographs taken, people coming to their table,
stopping to talk, asking about the gallery. Derek held
her closely while they danced, and when he led her back
to the table he stretched his arm along the back of her
chair.

The evening was half over, and Danni was searching
her mind for a reasonable excuse to suggest leaving, when
she became aware of Derek staring at two people who
stood behind them. Her polite smile faded as she turned
in her chair to see who they were, because Jackson North
stood there, stern and unsmiling, his companion beside
him.

North ignored Derek, directing his hard gaze at Danni.

'I hope you won't be making too late a night of it, Miss Paige. I like my assistants alert and ready for action, not trying to catch up for lost sleep.'

Incredulously Danni registered the acid tone in his voice. Now that his companion stood in the light Danni saw that she was lovely, smooth and blonde and elegant, her perfect figure draped in white crepe beaded in silver. She stood with cool assurance beside North, and Danni didn't need the faintly supercilious twist of her perfect red lips to tell her that the scarlet gown and glittering golden chains were not this beauty's idea of what the perfect assistant should wear.

Danni said with false brightness, 'I'm used to early rising, Mr North, no matter what time I get to bed,' and once again she had the feeling that whatever she said was going to sound faintly ridiculous. Why ever was she letting this man put her out of her stride?

Jackson North did not linger long enough at their table to be introduced around, although a few of the girls were preening themselves, ready to say hello to the great man. Danni felt the rustle of excitement, then the disappointment as North turned on his heel.

Derek was eager too, delighted to welcome a celebrity at his table. His smile had been over-eager if anything, and Danni watched it fade as North virtually ignored him except for a curt nod before he strode away, his companion beside him.

Derek's boyish face clouded. 'Who does he think he is, ordering you around like that?' He looked at Danni as if it were her fault. He wasn't exactly sulking but he was close to it, and Danni reluctantly allowed herself to be persuaded into staying more than an hour longer, although she was so weary now that dancing was an effort.

Derek hadn't planned to leave before the last dance. He wasn't happy, so on the way home Danni exerted herself to restore his good humour. After all he was her friend, and she didn't want to leave tomorrow with coolness between them. Gradually Derek responded but when she excused herself quickly at the gates of the caravan park, explaining she still had some packing to do, the petulance came back into his face.

He kissed her once, a cool kiss, before he asked, 'How big a crew is this fellow taking with him tomorrow?'

'I don't know. I didn't ask.'

Crew? She hadn't given that a thought. Maybe there would not be just the two of them after all. Her misgivings might be all in her imagination. Wouldn't there have to be another photographer, or a mechanic—somebody else beside the assistant who had let him down?

Relief made her feel warmer towards Derek. She hadn't really been fair to him, springing on him so suddenly the news that she planned to go travelling with a man she hardly knew. She returned his kiss with warmth, apologising for cutting the evening short; but when she bent to pick up her small gold clutch-purse from the floor of the car where it had fallen she straightened to find his arms waiting, uncomfortably close and eager, as if to make up for previous chilliness, and she muttered quickly, 'I'm sorry, Derek, I really am. But I have to go,' before she fled.

For some reason she didn't want anybody's arms around her tonight. She was edgy, her composure crumbling.

Behind her she heard Derek's voice. 'At least that bastard knows you're my girl.'

Danni walked softly into the caravan. Lilyan Paige lay very still in her bed. She looked to be asleep but Danni suspected she wasn't.

Quietly she took off the golden chains from around
her neck and pulled the scarlet dress over her shoulders.
She spent five minutes brushing the glitter out of her
hair, watching little specks of gold float down to the
floor, as if something magical might have happened to
her this evening, but Danni knew better. There had been
nothing magical at all.

She was caught in a web of circumstances that
threatened her with various possibilities, all of them om-
inous. Derek offended, Jackson North the unknown
quantity, arrogant and demanding...her evening hadn't
been exactly a Christmas party and tomorrow didn't look
like being much fun either.

Aching muscles reminded her of the long board ride
out to North's island, and she climbed thankfully into
bed and settled her head on the pillow. As she reached
out a hand to turn off the bedside light she found herself
hoping desperately that sleep would come quickly, but
instead she found herself staring into the darkness, her
head full of whirling questions, tantalising her because
they had no answers.

CHAPTER THREE

THERE were shadows under Danni's eyes next morning, the result of a tense and wakeful night. She could not have explained to anyone, least of all to herself, why she hovered so close to the reception area for most of the morning, inventing small errands that took her back and forth between their caravans and the store where the telephone waited for Jackson North's call.

Danni didn't doubt that he would ring, not even when half the morning passed without a call. She was well into packing her gear by that time, topping up the contents of her suitcase with the green skirt and the white top with its painted crab, adding a green sun-hat before she fastened it up and settled it near the door of the caravan.

From the doorway she saw the big four-wheel-drive vehicle swing into the caravan park, but it was only when the driver opened the door and stepped out that she realised North had arrived in person, and then of course there was no mistaking the powerful tanned figure.

She watched him stretch long arms and straighten his back, flexing his muscles like a cat waking after sunsleep. He must have made a long night of it, after all, Danni decided. Even from where she stood she could see the dark shadows around cheeks and jawline, so he obviously hadn't found time to shave.

Danni watched him with misgiving, because he didn't look around him with any of the interest of a man who hadn't seen it all before. Of course he must have inspected the whole property before he bought it, and that meant—that had to mean—Jay North had known exactly what he was buying and who he was dispossessing, and Danni gave an involuntary shiver. What an enemy...to remember for so long. It must have been deliberate, as Edwin had suggested. But whatever could the Paige family have done to his father to stir in him this incredible rancour?

Danni studied him covertly. He wore white slacks and a green polo shirt, so at first glance he could have been your average traveller, except for the attention-grabbing sign on the Range Rover, Jannorth Enterprises, in bright yellow, and when her uncle hurried out of the office Danni got ready to move but Uncle Edwin reached the four-wheel-drive before her.

'You looking for a site? Don't have much to offer, we're almost full, but I can fit you in.'

'Don't worry. That's not what I'm here for.'

Uncle Ed obviously hadn't read the sign on the Range Rover. He waved a hand along the driveway and North flicked a cursory glance over the clustered caravans.

'Yes. You certainly seem to be doing quite well.'

That was laughable. They were doing much better than 'quite well'. They were almost booked out. Danni would have called out to her uncle but North turned abruptly and walked towards the store. He didn't exactly brush the older man aside, but the effect was the same. He simply considered him of little importance and it showed.

Looking faintly confused, Edwin followed his visitor into the store and Danni almost ran the last few paces before she called from the doorway, 'Uncle Edwin, this is Mr North. Jackson North,' and the change in Edwin Paige's expression was almost comical.

He should have known, surely he must have recognised the dark man's face from the television screen, but he stood gaping until Lilyan spoke from the other side of the counter.

'Good morning. We were hoping to talk with you, Mr North.' She used her cool-lady voice and Jay asked softly,

'Mrs Paige? Mrs Ryan Paige?' with a faint raising of his eyebrows as if she was not what he expected.

Then he moved across the room to the counter, leaving Danni to trail after him, which of course was just what he intended.

Jay North's presence in the park acted like a magnet. Gregg appeared from the laundry where he had been fixing a washing-machine, and he stared at his former idol with undisguised interest until Danni made reluctant introductions. Several people strolled by, pretending to look casual, as if they had not come for a look at the star, but Danni pushed the door half-shut behind her and there were no interruptions.

If it had been anyone else standing there before the half-circle of accusing Paiges this could have looked like an inquisition, but the tall dark man simply by standing there with so much indifference seemed to deflect the accusations before they could be spoken. He turned calmly to Danni.

'I have to leave earlier than I intended. I plan to take off early this afternoon. Can you be ready?'

'I'll have to be, won't I? You're giving the orders.'

Danni's sharp retort made her uncle blink, even Gregg looked slightly startled, but Lilyan asked steadily, 'I'm sure you won't mind, Mr North, if we ask for some details of your itinerary. You realise we need to get in touch with Danni if the need arises. How long do you expect to be away?'

'Two weeks. Maybe a little longer. I'm afraid I can't pin myself down to exact locations at any given time, but I'll leave you a rough outline of the ground we're covering. We'll be travelling north through Central Queensland, then west and south-west. I've covered most of the ground before, but some of our film was damaged and we need replacements.'

'How far?' Already Gregg was wide-eyed. He edged closer.

'Heaven knows. As far as it takes to get what we want. Among other things we have some good news for an old battler who owns a run-down pub and store way out in the middle of nowhere. With any luck it should all be completed fairly simply but I've learned to allow for the unexpected.'

Edwin Paige coughed and began, 'Now, see here——' but Danni interrupted quickly, 'It's all right, Uncle Ed.'

The dark man scarcely paused before he moved to the doorway. The smile he offered Lilyan was a token one, a faint movement of the lips with no warmth in it at all; Uncle Ed and Gregg didn't even get that, just a curt nod as Jay took Danni's arm and led her outside.

'Tell me what you've packed.'

'Everything I'm likely to need. You didn't expect me to bring any ballgowns, did you?'

'Don't get smart with me.' His voice was grim, unbending.

'Shall I need my typewriter?'

'Only if you prefer it. I'll have a small portable machine with me.'

Danni outlined the contents of her case and carry-all and he nodded. 'OK.' His smile was wintry. 'Don't bother about money.' The irony was back in his expression. 'All expenses paid.'

'Thank you, sir. You really are too kind.'

He didn't find that amusing. The glance he gave her was glacial.

'Whether I am kind or not will depend entirely on how you do your work.'

He emphasised the word 'work' as if to stress their relationship was a work one only, and that made Danni feel easier, but unaccountably slightly offended.

'I'll do the best I can. You needn't worry about me not trying to earn my keep.'

He answered cynically, 'I'm sure you will. There's a lot hanging on it, isn't there?'

Danni knew he was thinking of Uncle Edwin and his apparently prosperous caravan park, reminding her that its future depended on her.

She watched him step into his vehicle and drive away, aware that she in her turn was being watched speculatively by a small group of people on the other side of the driveway.

When Danni went back into the office Uncle Edwin was talking volubly. He had been rather subdued while the other man was present; now he addressed Danni with belligerence.

'Damn cheek! He comes here and talks to us as if we don't matter a hoot.' He turned to Danni. 'Looks as if your mother's opal wasn't enough for the North family. He's come back for more. Greedy lot, the Norths. His father was a schemer and I'll bet the son's no better.'

Danni asked quickly, 'What did you say about an opal?' and her uncle looked vaguely discomfited.

'Someone ought to tell you,' he mumbled doggedly. His round pink face grew rosier.

'Your father dug out a really good stone at Coober Pedy. Not a very big piece but full of fire. I can see it now. Ryan had it made into a necklace and brooch for your mother, only that scoundrel North finished up with it. Kept it till the day he died. We never saw it again.'

Edwin Paige jabbed the counter angrily. 'Bet that son of his could tell you where it is now. He's a shady operator, that one.'

Danni searched her mother's face. 'You never told us anything about opals, Mums,' and Lilyan sighed.

'It isn't important.' She turned to her brother-in-law. 'Let's not talk about it, Edwin. It really doesn't matter, and talking won't alter anything.'

'Was it valuable?' Gregg had been listening wide-eyed but nobody answered his question, and cold fingers seemed to be touching Danni's heart. If the stone was valuable then Gardiner North could have been a thief. Danni considered his son arrogant and pushy, definitely non-desirable, but this was something different. It was theft. And if he was the son of a double-dealer, then maybe Jackson North had learned a few tricks from his father, and where did that leave her? Alone in the outback with a man whose motives were questionable and whose word could mean nothing at all?

Her mother said with unexpected strength in her voice, 'Gregg, the subject is closed,' and Danni and Gregg exchanged faint grimaces before Gregg moved away to finish his work in the laundry.

Danni went along the shelves in the store collecting the last few items she needed to take with her, and to her surprise her fingers were steady, although her thoughts were whirling. Her only misgivings about the trip until now had been focused entirely on the fact that Jay North was obviously a virile male and he might have considered a feminine travelling companion fair game on a journey such as this. Now something uglier and definitely more dangerous had been introduced. Could that be why the man had lashed out at her so quickly when she used the expression 'dirty tricks' out on his island? Maybe dirty tricks had made him famous and successful. A new and definitely disturbing dimension had been introduced into an already daunting journey, and Danni struggled to hide her misgivings as she caught her mother and uncle watching her, both with concerned faces.

She dropped her collection of small articles on the counter. Toothpaste, sunscreen cream, tissues, a few other useful items.

'There you are. I'll pay for that little lot and maybe I'll be able to persuade the Big Star to reimburse me.' But she was the only one smiling. Her mother looked pointedly at Uncle Edwin.

'Are you sure we should let her go, Ed?'

Some impulse she could not explain made Danni stare hard at her uncle. 'I suppose I could call it off, if you think I should,' she said, and Edwin blinked, and wavered, his eyes sliding away from hers.

'Unfortunately, it seems the only way. This bloke isn't ready to do favours for nothing and I suppose you're old enough to look after yourself. Looks as if you're doing the right thing.'

'I'm sure I am.' She hoped that sounded positive. She had a sneaky feeling her uncle would have been horrified if she cancelled the trip now, and she really didn't blame him. Edwin had looked after the family ever since her father's death some years ago, holding them together. Now he needed her to do something for him, and it shouldn't be too much to expect. His whole future, and theirs, was in jeopardy, and he would be foolish to dissuade her now.

Lilyan murmured a protesting 'Danni...' and Danni reassured her. 'I'm looking forward to the work, truly. Just think of all the information I'll absorb.' She bundled her purchases into a plastic bag and almost ran with them to the caravan.

Uncle Edwin liked substantial meals. 'None of this sandwiches and coffee stuff,' he always requested, and after she finished packing Danni set about preparing what would be her last family meal for at least two weeks.

She took barramundi steaks out of the freezer and put them in the electric frying pan before she made the salads, and all the time her mind nagged her with questions she had no hope of answering.

At lunch, Danni toyed with the fish and salad on her plate, making a pretence of eating, and Lilyan did the same. Only Gregg and his uncle ate heartily, and afterwards Gregg hovered around waiting for North to arrive.

Danni looked at the shadows under her eyes and added extra blusher to her cheeks to disguise her wan appearance. She changed into white cotton slacks and loose jacket, with a rose-coloured camisole top to throw more colour over her pale features. She let her hair hang loose to her shoulders, and Gregg assured her she looked stunning.

It seemed important to him that she make a good impression and she snapped sharply, 'It doesn't matter how I look,' but he grinned and walked a few yards away, whistling.

Danni was almost at screaming point when the four-wheel-drive returned to the park. This time it had a heavily loaded pack-rack on top and its rear was piled high with equipment, including a small motorcycle.

Jay called 'Ready?' looking in Danni's direction, and Gregg leaped to pick up her luggage and hand it over. Jay was clean-shaven now. He didn't waste time, just pushing Danni's things among the other equipment and handing Lilyan a slip of paper.

'That's our itinerary, as far as I can tell. You understand it has to be flexible but I've outlined general directions. We're not blazing any new trails. Nothing dangerous.'

Lilyan held the paper in her hand. 'I'm delighted to hear that.' But she didn't look all that confident. Gregg peered at it over her shoulder.

'Are you going to see any crocodiles?'

Jay shook his head. 'We're not going far enough north for that, I'm afraid.' But Gregg's expression remained wistful.

'Wish I could come with you. I'd like to see everything, I've always wanted to explore.'

Something in Gregg's expression must have reached the dark man. He said in an almost human voice, 'You'll probably see it all in good time, if you want it badly enough.'

That would be his philosophy, of course. If you want it, go out and get it, but Danni was careful to mask her thoughts. There was enough antagonism between them already.

Gregg asked a few more questions and North answered them as he strapped down the last of the luggage, but when Edwin took the piece of paper from Lilyan and remarked querulously that it seemed vague and not very informative North's expression tightened and he answered shortly that he couldn't tell Edwin what he didn't know himself.

He had a very intimidating scowl and he must be tired, because his cheekbones showed sharply in the tanned face and the tightened lips gave his face a taciturnity that made Edwin step away, but Gregg wasn't abashed.

'Should we call you Jay,' he asked the dark man innocently, 'like they do on the telly?'

So the charisma was coming over, and the charm, and Gregg had already forgotten his disillusionment with his hero. He was showing all the signs of hero-worship restored and North said indifferently, 'Call me Jay if you want to, until I change my mind.'

Gregg's face brightened. 'Don't suppose you need another relief driver? I mean, Danni's OK, but she's a girl.'

Lilyan made a small helpless movement as if she would have hushed her son but Jay's expression remained cryptic.

'Not this trip, thanks. I'll just have to put up with Danni being a girl.'

The boy grinned. 'Well, you know where I am. If you need me, just call. I could easily join you.'

So much for Gregg's disappointment in his hero. It hadn't taken much for the other man to regain himself a fan.

But Lilyan was slower to relent. Charisma or not, Jackson North would have to prove himself. She watched him gravely as he went about the business of checking the gear in the pack-rack on the roof, and when he finished she said in a quiet voice, 'Mr North, we expect you to bring Danni safely back to us,' and to Danni's surprise Jackson turned to her with a whimsical smile touching the corners of his mouth.

'I'll do that, Mrs Paige, don't worry.'

Rather than turn the heavily loaded vehicle, North drove the length of the park, his keen gaze not missing anything this time. As they passed the lagoon Danni ventured, 'What about the rest of your crew? Do we meet them on the road?'

He was watching the ibis, slowing down as they wandered close to the edge of the drive, and he was in no hurry to answer.

He kept her waiting until Danni thought he intended dodging the question then he said softly, 'The rest of our crew is behind us.'

There was no other vehicle in sight. Danni scanned the empty driveway. Then a faint movement behind her seat attracted her attention. A small dog, a terrier with a grey and tan curly coat, tilted his head curiously as he studied Danni out of bright eyes. Jay followed her glance.

'That's Lionel. Lion for short but only when he knows you better. We'll have to wait and see if you're accepted as friend.'

He leaned heavily on that word *if*, as though he considered it unlikely, and Danni snapped,

'Are you telling me we are on our own, just the two of us?'

'As you knew perfectly well from the beginning.' North's voice was dangerously soft. 'How many people would you imagine?'

Of course she had known all along, Danni admitted reluctantly to herself, but it didn't make her feel any more comfortable to have the man spell it out.

They passed the office and Gregg and Lilyan and Edwin stood outside waving. It probably looked a cosy scene, a happy send-off, but Danni saw that her mother clutched the piece of paper in her hand, her expression tense. She could have been farewelling her daughter on the way to join the *Titanic*, that was what her expression said.

They were approaching the gateway when Derek's silver-grey Falcon stopped suddenly in front of them, barring their exit. Jackson brought the four-wheel-drive to a sudden halt, muttering something inaudible. He wasn't pleased and he didn't care who knew it.

As Derek scrambled out of the driver's seat he received a baleful glare followed by a terse, 'We're in a hurry. Do you mind?'

He ignored that, stamped around to where Danni sat, and glowered at her.

'Mother tells me we've run short of those shirts you paint. There isn't one on the shelves. What are we supposed to do?'

'They're in the store-room, bottom cupboard, right-hand side. Your mother should know that. I told her.'

Derek's jaw tightened. 'You're going, then?' His eyes were angry. 'You're really going off heavens knows where with this man?'

'I'm doing a job.' Danni tried to make him feel better. 'Two or three weeks' work, that's all.'

Derek didn't turn and say to Jackson North, as Danni's family had done, 'Bring her back safely'. He thrust his lower jaw out and glowered at Danni, as if she were deserting him with work undone, and that wasn't true.

She said with spurious brightness, 'I haven't left anything outstanding as far as I know, and Fiona will take my place in the gallery. She promised.'

Derek grunted. He shot Jackson North a look of enmity before turning on his heel and getting back into his car, and the face he turned to Danni as he moved away was unhappy and accusing. Danni didn't blame him. After all, he didn't know that there was a special reason for her taking this job with North.

She watched Derek's car turn off the road ahead of them and take a short cut back to the gallery, and as it disappeared among the overhanging trees that screened the side track Danni found herself with an almost desperate feeling of being cut off from everything and everybody familiar to her.

For the first time in her life she felt really lonely, not certain she could handle the situation in which she found herself. She had never been short on confidence, never really had need to feel deeply insecure in spite of Ed's business failures. They had always moved on to something else.

Yet sitting here with the swarthy man beside her, his legs stretched comfortably in front of him, relaxed as if he felt well in control of the situation, Danni found herself wondering exactly what sort of predicament she could be gettng herself into, and whether she would be able to cope with whatever turned up, now that she was going so far from everything that was familiar.

CHAPTER FOUR

THE atmosphere inside the four-wheel-drive grew chillier. Danni kept as much space between herself and Jay North as the front seat allowed her. Pride demanded she did not huddle in the corner, but she did the best she could to keep them well apart and still retain her dignity.

She knew the dark man was aware of the careful distance she kept between them, although he gave no sign. As they neared the highway the dog Lionel crawled between them, curled discreetly close to his master. They were travelling west through bright sunlight when North broke the silence.

'Caring fellow, your boyfriend.'

He dropped the comment without looking at her. The underlying sarcasm in his cold voice did not escape Danni, and when she did not answer he shot her a quick hard look from under level brows before he went on, 'He showed a really touching concern for your welfare, I must say.'

Danni stiffened. 'How would you know?'

He increased speed to pass a slow-moving vehicle ahead of them and as they straightened he added, 'What are those shirts he's talking about?'

Smarting from his sarcasm, Danni answered resentfully, 'They don't concern you.'

Momentarily he took his attention away from the road to give her another sharp piercing look from glacial grey eyes.

'Anything that you are and do is of concern to me for the next few weeks, Danielle. Don't think it isn't. Who

55

you are and what you are is of vital importance to me for that short period of time. After that——' He shrugged his shoulders.

They had reached the highway now and he let several cars pass before he swung on to it, then he said coldly, 'Now, about those shirts. Are you tailoress as well as scriptwriter and typist?'

'No. I don't make them. I paint designs on them,' Danni snapped at him resentfully.

He raised eyebrows in a gesture of mockery. 'Dispersing your talents, aren't you? And what's your arrangement with the solicitous boyfriend?' He slanted a swift glance at the fingers of her left hand. 'Not engaged and hiding the ring, I hope.'

Danni maintained stubborn silence and he gave a short hard laugh before returning his attention to the road.

'All right. Keep your secrets. But don't try anything underhand, Danielle. The Paige family doesn't stand too well with me, and by God I won't stand for any tricks.'

Dirty tricks, he meant. Danni glanced at his hard strong fingers curved around the steering-wheel. Tough, ruthless fingers. Once again she had the cold finger of foreboding touching her spine. What on earth had she got herself into?

If only she could have slept last night she probably wouldn't have had this dreary feeling dragging her spirits down. She only hoped Jackson North hadn't noticed the shadows around her eyes. She slumped into her corner, letting her eyelids droop, and she was half asleep later when they left the highway and turned on to a wide country road, and North pulled up on the gravel verge.

'All right,' he told Danni briskly, 'let's see you begin to earn your keep.'

Danni stared at him numbly. 'How do I do that?'

He leaned across and opened her door. 'Time for your driving-lesson.'

'Oh, well, why didn't you say so?'

She could have had a headache, a small nagging heaviness throbbed behind her eyes, but the need to sharpen her senses pulled her together. The four-wheel-drive wasn't all that difficult to handle, on this terrain not much different from her own small car. A few instructions and Danni was on her way.

At first her companion sat attentively beside her, then Danni felt him relax.

He reached under the seat and pulled out a document in a cardboard folder and when he became immersed in reading Danni became aware of an utterly unreasonable lightness of heart. Her driving couldn't be all that bad. Even the weariness seemed to have lifted and she spun along the country road, actually enjoying her first experience with the heavy vehicle.

They had left the coast far behind and were close to the mountain ranges when Jay instructed her to stop. As she re-settled herself in the passenger seat he said negligently, 'You'll be pleased to know you've passed the first test. It remains to be seen how you'll go with the next.'

Danni stared at him indignantly. 'I'm not here to pass tests,' she snapped. 'I'm here to do a job as your assistant.'

She sat up straight in her seat, waiting for Jackson North to drive off, and when he did not move she stared at him defiantly, and he reached over and flicked her cheek with one hard finger.

'Oh yes, you are Danni,' he said softly. 'You are here to do whatever I say and to pass any tests I choose to set you, and don't think that you aren't. I didn't tell you I was an easy boss to get along with.'

'No, you didn't.' Danni didn't have to worry about colour in her cheeks now. They were flaming. Tiredness vanished. She was blazing with anger.

'Mr North——' and he interrupted,

'Jay. Call me Jay. As our situation is about to become so intimate I prefer you use my name—'

'Our position is not—repeat not—going to become intimate, Mr—Jay, if that's what you want. And your tests don't intimidate me. I'll do the best work I can for you and when it's over I intend to hold you to your promise. Don't think I won't.'

He gave her a quizzical look.

'The first thing you'll have to do is put a brake on that quick temper if you hope to keep the job. Hasn't anybody ever told you that bad temper is a total waste of energy?'

Only afterwards did it occur to Danni that he had neatly avoided her reference to his promise. He selected a cassette tape and inserted it. Classical music...Rachmaninov. What had she expected? Danni didn't know. She was quite sure this man was full of surprises.

She watched his hands on the wheel, an expensive-looking watch on one sun-tanned wrist, a fine gold chain on the other, and before she knew it she had a moment of wayward wondering whether the luscious blonde from the dinner-dance had given it to him. She averted her gaze quickly, tried to look interested in the scenery.

A little later he slowed down and reached over to the rear to produce a bag filled with fruit which he put on the seat between them.

'Help yourself if you fancy some nourishment.' He chose a plump banana and Danni helped herself, as directed, to a bunch of grapes. When she had finished eating he nodded towards the folder of script he had been reading while she drove.

'You'd better read that as we go along. I haven't included the whole script, only the scenes that require ad-

ditions and editing, but it will give you some idea of
what the documentary is all about.'

Danni checked the synopsis inside the front cover.
'You've covered a lot of territory.'

'Yes, we have. There's quite a bit of it we shan't be
touching this time. Our first call is on an elderly
Aboriginal friend of mine who's been ill. He has a
tumour on one leg, and our "white man's medicine"
has pronounced it malignant and incurable. Amputation has been suggested but he's resisting. When I in-
terviewed him last he'd "gone bush"—back to his tribal
land and his people—to see whether tribal man's magic
can do any better before he makes a final decision.'

Danni asked quietly, 'If the growth is malignant
shouldn't it be removed quickly?'

Jay nodded thoughtfully. 'It's usually advisable but
Tomi Ollerah decided to take a gamble. Mind you——
' his lips quirked '—he didn't altogether turn his back
on white man's medicine. He's had ray treatment and
some chemotherapy and whatever else the hospital had
to offer. But he's an old man and I suppose amputation
seemed horribly drastic——'

He let the sentence hang uncompleted, giving all his
attention to the road. They were climbing steeply, around
spiralling mountain roads, and Danni looked down into
deep gullies where bougainvillas grew wild among the
greenery, making vivid splashes of purple and crimson
below them.

She turned her attention to the script until they reached
the top of the mountains, and on the other side a different world greeted them.

A storm-threatening sky faced them, full of swirling
inky clouds, and in the distance Danni caught the fierce
white flash of lightning, heard the rumble of thunder.
Jay pulled up and checked the tarpaulin over the pack-
rack and the dog Lionel made small whimpering sounds.

'He doesn't like thunderstorms and I think we're headed for a beauty.' Jay grimaced at the dog. 'His name may be Lion but he's a real chicken when lightning flashes and thunder roars.'

'So am I,' Danni confessed without stopping to think.

'That so? Then I'll have two of you to look after. That should prove interesting.'

Jay was staring ahead as they descended the twisting road but there was enough suggestion in his voice for Danni to retort quickly, 'I can take care of myself, thank you.'

'That's something we'll have to discover.' The words were spoken so softly that Danni hardly picked them up, but they left her with a feeling of disquiet.

She concentrated on the script, and when rain began beating on the windscreen mentally reviewed her luggage. It looked like being weather for gumboots and rainwear, and she was thankful she had stowed wet-weather wear in her suitcase.

Once, Jay glanced at her quizzically as if he had tuned in to her musing. 'Don't worry. Deluge today, sunshine tomorrow. If we're lucky.'

If...Danni went back to the script but as daylight faded she let the folder drop on to her lap and leaned her head back against the seat. Reaction must be setting in; she felt jumpy now as well as tired. What were they going to do in the rain? And what was going to happen to her out there in the wildness that lay ahead, miles away from everything and everybody she knew?

The man sitting so nonchalantly beside her had offered no papers, no written cancellation of his notice to her family that he required their park land. He'd given a verbal undertaking only, and as he had said to Danni out on the island, how much was that worth?

They had left the mountains behind them, and fierce flashes of lightning and thunderclaps sounding perilously close made Danni open her eyes apprehensively. Jay flicked her a swift glance before putting his foot down a little harder on the accelerator.

'Won't be driving much farther. Something tells me you really aren't a storm lady.'

Danni said warily, 'I don't object to minor upheavals but this one is a bit out of my line.'

'You surprise me. I imagined you'd relish a bit of excitement.'

'It depends on the flavour. This one isn't to my taste.' She shivered as the dusk was split by an almost blinding flash of light, and the man actually laughed.

'Not to worry.' His teeth glinted white in the shadows. 'We shan't be pitching tents in this downpour. There's a wayside café with overnight flats somewhere in the next mile or so. We'll see what they can do for us. We may even get a meal.'

Strange how remote a person could look, profile etched against gathering darkness as they drove. He sat back easily, one hand on the wheel, the other lying on his own thigh as he concentrated on the driving rain. Remote, and yet aware.

Of course he knew she was staring at him. Quickly, Danni redirected her attention to the storm. A person could become extremely uncomfortable, thrust into the company of a man who had more than his share of intuition. Instinct told her surely that Jay picked up things other people might miss, and the charisma that helped him so easily charm Gregg out of his reservations was a dangerous power, something she would have to beware of. His kind of man used people, and used them very deftly and without a conscience, she was sure of it.

Deep in uneasy musing, Danni scarcely noticed as they turned into a run-off alongside the road. She opened her eyes to see the dim shapes of petrol pumps outside a garage and a dimly-lit café showed one man sitting at a table in an otherwise deserted dining-room.

Jay climbed out, hunching his shoulders, running through the rain. He came back dangling a key.

'We're in luck. Got the last available flat.'

The last flat, he said. Surely he wasn't expecting her to share with him!

Without another glance towards Danni, Jay slowly edged their vehicle towards a rickety double gate on the other side of the garage. A man in yellow waterproofs carrying a torch pushed open the gate and pointed them into an open space, where a line of small wooden units stood at the far end.

'Middle one, number seven,' he shouted before ambling away and Jay nodded and began driving slowly through the puddles of rain.

Outside the door of number seven he pulled up, leaned over and dragged out two waterproof sheets and a torch. He handed Danni one of the sheets.

'Cover yourself and follow me.'

He squelched across puddles to the doorway and Danni followed dubiously. Jay opened the door and switched on the light. The room looked surprisingly comfortable. It held one double bed and a large divan, with a separated section at the rear obviously holding shower and toilet facilities. Along one side wall a wooden polished bench held hot-water jug, radio, and a tray with cups and saucers beside a small refrigerator. Casually Jay dropped his torch on to the divan.

'Better mark my territory, I suppose,' he announced ironically, as Danni hovered just inside the doorway.

'Are we both sleeping in this room? Is that your plan?'

'Unless you prefer to stay out in the rain, which I can't allow, because the last thing I want is an assistant with pneumonia. Don't worry about my comfort——' the irony became more marked '—this divan is luxury com-

pared with some of the places I've slept. So freshen
yourself up if you want,' he nodded towards the
bathroom, 'and don't take too long. They're getting us
a meal.'

Don't take too long... Danni was in no mood to be
hustled. She lingered, brushing her hair, repairing lip-
stick, then realised he might get impatient and leave her
there and that was the last thing she wanted, to be left
alone with this horrible storm rattling all around her.

When she hurried out into the main room Jay handed
her the waterproof and grinned sardonically as she followed him meekly to be driven to the café.

Inside the café he looked at her across the red and
white gingham-covered table. 'Tell me about yourself.'

'Why should I?'

'Because I need to know. I don't go travelling about
the country with just anybody.'

'It's a bit late to think of that now.' Danni clamped
down simmering indignation. 'There isn't much to tell,'
she countered. 'I haven't been nearly as busy as you
have.' In case that sounded like a snipe she added hurriedly, 'I don't travel about the country much at all, not
the outback. I'm saving my money to go overseas.'

'What's overseas that's so special?'

'I don't know.' She didn't intend spilling all her hopes
and dreams to a man she scarcely knew and didn't like
anyway.

His lips curled. 'You don't know. That's a hell of a
way to plan your life. Sounds as if you haven't started
to live yet. Hadn't you better get busy and start organising? There must be a lot of things you haven't tried
yet, by the sound of it.'

It was only now, in the compelling presence of the
man who leaned back watching her, that Danni realised
that her plans for the future were really nebulous. She

hadn't worked them out in detail, they hadn't any exact shape at all.

Sometimes she had imagined a need to travel, and there was a nice little nest-egg in her bank deposit book; now she wondered whether that was merely an excuse to break out from the restrictions of the life she led with her family, and that shocked her, making her feel faintly disloyal.

In the muted light from the café ceiling she studied the tough lines on the face of the man who shared her table. It could have been fatigue that tightened the muscles of the strong jaw and accentuated two deep lines from the strong nose to the mouth, but in the unflattering illumination it was a graven face, harsh and unforgiving, and Danni said uneasily, 'All right. Since we're exchanging information, what do you do besides making documentaries?'

'Don't change the subject. We haven't finished with you yet. What exactly do you do with your time?' A grim smile flickered across the taciturn features. 'Apart from occasional visits to television production studios and other people's private islands.'

Danni shook away annoyance. This was no time to quarrel. The solitary man at a nearby table was looking their way with obvious interest, staring at Jay as if he hoped to attract his attention.

Danni watched Jay offer him the tersest of nods, a pushing-away gesture that should have sent the man back to his coffee, but seemed only to please him remarkably.

Danni said, 'I do some freelance writing. I've had a few short stories published and some newspaper articles in one of our local papers. I help in the caravan park.' She allowed herself a faint smile. 'I'm a really mean mechanic with a difficult washing-machine. And I make those T-shirts and tops for Derek and help out in his gallery sometimes.'

'Ah yes—Derek. I thought he might get a mention. So you're really everybody's little helper?'

He drawled the words slowly but they were an insult. They made her sound ineffectual, a girl who didn't know what she wanted or where she was going, and wasn't bothering about it too much.

She said stiffly, 'Derek can sell all the souvenirs I make. He wants me to do it full-time.'

The grey eyes glittered. 'We keep coming back to him, don't we? The suspicious boyfriend.'

'What did you expect him to think?'

North leaned a little farther back into the shadows, but he didn't hesitate. 'I wouldn't expect him to think anything. He's not my business. But if I were his lady I'd like to believe he'd accept that I'd taken on another bit of freelance work for a couple of weeks and I could be trusted to handle it without any suspicious and dirty suggestions from him. You're not stupid, I hope, and you're not a child either, are you?'

'No, to both.' But he was making her feel like a child. He must understand, a man with his ego, that he wasn't just any man. He was something out of the common, and she wouldn't have told him for worlds, but most men would have been jealous and uneasy to have their girlfriend jaunting off with Jackson North anywhere, working or not.

Danni was relieved when a cheerful girl brought their rib steaks with vegetables and hot garlic bread. The cook came from the kitchen to see that everything met with Jay's approval. No doubt about it, the man had impact. They were falling over themselves to please him.

Danni didn't want to talk any more. She felt she had lost momentum, as if every movement, even eating, was an effort.

The stress of the last two days was all piling up on her; the letter from Jay North's lawyers, the late night, the cooling of her friendship with Derek, they had all shaken her security. All she really wanted to do now was sleep, then maybe tomorrow she could put herself together.

They ate in silence until their plates were cleared and the waitress brought coffee, then Jay said unexpectedly, 'Sorry I can't produce a bottle of wine to lift your spirits.'

'I don't need wine.' That was the last thing she needed in this mood, a few glasses of wine to make her light-headed. 'The coffee will do nicely.'

But there were tremors running down her fingers and that was unusual for Danni. She always had control, no matter how tired she might be. She put her cup down quickly, before she challenged,

'I notice you aren't telling me about yourself, or am I supposed to know it all from the television screen?'

He laughed suddenly, a clear spontaneous laugh that banished the hard lines from his face.

'Are you trying to put me down?' His eyes gleamed at her. 'Or are you asking if what you see is what you get?'

He amused himself with that while Danni sipped more coffee, then he said suddenly, 'I think I'll keep myself as a surprise. Perhaps after our travelling is finished you'll be able to fill in the picture for yourself.'

Danni put down her cup with a clatter. 'You mean I'm snoopy and I shouldn't ask questions?' she flared.

'Not necessarily. I may even let you share one or two of my innermost secrets as we go along, but then again I may not. It depends on what develops between us.'

She didn't like the suggestive glint in his eyes, nor the ironic lift of the straight black brows.

'Nothing is going to develop between us.'

Danni couldn't have sounded more positive. He quirked the eyebrows even higher at her vehemence. Then he ordered coolly, 'Drink up your coffee. Lionel is probably starving. I've ordered something for him from the kitchen.'

The girl behind the counter was signalling Jay, holding up a paper plate wrapped in silver foil.

'Doggie-bag,' she chuckled as she handed it to Jay cheerfully. 'Hope your little fellow enjoys it.'

They were certainly doing their best to please. The girl's smile was radiant, pure 'apple for the teacher', as she watched Jay settle the doggie-bag on the palm of his hand. He was charismatic, all right, Mr Charisma himself, despite the grimness that fell like a shadow over his features when he was not animated. He had charm and power, and he undoubtedly knew how to use both.

She tried to tell herself it was because of the television exposure—he was Jay North the celebrity—but honesty compelled Danni to decide that whoever he was, whatever he was doing, Jay would always have this strong presence, this abominable nerve that took other people's responses for granted.

He was smiling faintly at the girl now, a clever smile with just a hint of hauteur, and she stood gazing blissfully after him as he headed, doggie-bag in hand, towards the door. She offered a smile to Danni also, but it was different, polite and friendly with a hint of envy.

Jay stood aside for Danni to precede him through the doorway and something in his careful expression told Danni instantly that once again he was tuned in to her thoughts, and she hunched her shoulders as she walked into the rain towards their parked vehicle.

OK. So he had presence, and he was shrewd, and he knew how to read people. He turned heads. She would have to make sure he didn't turn hers.

Lionel sniffed joyfully at the parcel and Jay teased, 'Another couple of minutes, mate,' before he put the key in the ignition and drove back through the rickety gateway to their flat. He pulled out a small rug and arranged it underneath the vehicle.

'Lionel sleeps outside. He's on guard duty,' he explained and the dog gave a couple of crisp barks before hurling himself at the food spread out for him.

Jay collected the cameras and their overnight bags, then handed Danni a small portable typewriter.

'How do you feel about tackling four or five pages of typing? Can you manage it, or are you still catching up after your heavy night last night?'

Danni thought she detected a cynical undertone in his voice, but she ignored it. She couldn't let him know how tired she was, knowing it could be misconstrued.

She was dismayed to feel her heart pounding erratically as Jay turned the key and opened the door of the flat. He clicked on the light and, pretending a confidence she did not feel, Danni walked inside, careful not to brush against him as she passed. He followed her, soft-footed on the carpeted floor, so that she gasped when she half turned and there he was, quite close to her, almost touching. He took the typewriter out of her hand.

'I'll give you the pages I'd like you to alter, then we'd better have an early night.' He moved away, just far enough to arrange the typewriter on the bench. 'You're welcome to sit up and read a bit more of the script if you want, but we have a long way to go tomorrow, so I've ordered breakfast for six o'clock.'

He was unzipping his overnight bag. 'If you want to shower first, feel free.'

Danni shook her head. 'You've done most of the driving. I'll type while you shower.'

Of course he knew exactly what she was thinking. He thoroughly understood her tactics. If he showered first and was tired enough after the packing and the long drive maybe he would be in bed when she came out from her own shower. With a little luck he might even be asleep.

The sharp, clever eyes narrowed and the faintest of grins tilted the corners of the sensuous mouth.

'Have it your way. Here are my notes.'

Jay seemed a long time in the bathroom. The pungent fragrance of some toiletry floated through the half-closed door.

Danni applied herself to typing the few pages he had given her, working out the jigsaw of alterations. His writing was clear and sharp with strong downward strokes, his narrative crisp and vivid. She re-typed the pages without much trouble, leaving them beside the typewriter to check if he felt like it.

She noted thankfully that the divan had a supply of pillows, sheets and blankets, and decided to let him claim what he wanted. If he kept his word and settled for the divan she would take the double bed.

When he emerged from the shower Jay wore short pyjamas only, the top carelessly unbuttoned, and Danni averted her eyes quickly, but not before she had noticed the luxuriant growth of thick black curls on his chest and upper arms still faintly damp from the shower. The dark hair on his head was a mass of undisciplined curls and he walked to the wall-mirror and combed it into some sort of order; his air of careless indifference didn't fool Danni one bit.

She knew he was aware of every move she made, and chewed her lower lip hesitantly, because she had intended saying lightly, 'I'd better say goodnight in case you're asleep when I come back from the bathroom,' and suddenly those words seemed quite ridiculous and even faintly hysterical.

She knew exactly the look he would have given her so she said nothing, just fled into the annexe clutching her white cotton nightshirt, her toilet bag and a coloured towelling jacket.

She took her time about showering, dallying about brushing her hair and creaming her skin, taking more time and care than usual, not to impress the man outside but because she needed to delay the moment of her return. It seemed a trifle cowardly, but she was weary and tense after the storm, her confidence shaken, and she patted faintly scented talc over her body until she could tell herself hopefully that Jay should be half asleep and she could go quietly to bed unobserved.

She could have saved herself the trouble. Jay had taken the divan for himself all right, but he had placed the pillows at the strategic end so that he could lie watching her from the shadows as she prepared for bed. It was a creepy feeling, the rain drumming on the roof, the occasional rumble of thunder, and maybe it was only her own imagination that he was watching her, because he had turned off all but the wall light over the bench and the typewriter, and she wasn't really certain that he had his eyes open. That dark face was full of lines and shadows, and beneath the harsh strong brows his eyes were in hooded secrecy, maybe the lids closed entirely, maybe half closed and observant, as her over-tense nerves suggested.

He had left the script on the bench and Danni picked it up as she passed. Perhaps she should do the right thing and familiarise herself with the places they were heading for. She turned off the bench light, removed her towelling jacket, and put on the overhead lamp above her own bed.

She had settled herself in bed and opened the folder when Jay spoke.

'You're an accurate typist, Danielle, thank heavens.'

The words came softly but they jolted Danni because she had been just about ready to decide Jay was asleep.

When she made no answer he added conversationally, 'I wonder whether you excel equally at all your other activities.'

Danni sat up straighter. 'If that's a suggestive remark I don't appreciate it.' There was something taunting about the soft laughter that followed.

'Get back to your work like a good little girl.'

Jay rolled over, the divan creaked. 'As I told you, we're travelling north and farther inland tomorrow to see my Aboriginal friend, Tomi Ollerah. Might I suggest you read pages nineteen to thirty, if you can stay awake that long. That should cover it.'

Dutifully, Danni turned the pages, her eyelids heavy. She shouldn't have picked up the script in the first place but Jay had left it lying there as if he wished her to look it over before she went to sleep and she didn't want to seem uninterested.

Now here she was, bent over the folder, unaccountably nervous, not really absorbing everything she read, because instinct warned her the man on the divan was far from asleep.

Defensively she rolled on to her side, presenting him with a view of the back of her head should he open his eyes, and she was actually immersed in the script when his voice spoke softly, far too close for her peace of mind.

'Anything you don't understand?'

Danni jerked to attention. Jay North stood beside her bed, not far from the shoulder she had turned to hide herself from him. Danni twisted quickly, not stopping to use reason but shocked into some kind of manic and primitive reaction that set her hurtling out of bed, grabbing the towelling jacket, throwing it over her desperately and heading for the door. All this without making any conscious decision at all.

Jay watched her, frowning horribly. 'You're a touchy damn doll, you are. Heaven preserve me from temperamental females,' and as she fumbled clumsily with the door-handle he bit out, 'Where the hell do you think you're going? Out into the storm?'

'It's preferable.' She was almost in tears, the built-up tensions suddenly betraying her, shattering self-control.

Even as she turned on him, some detached part of her mind and reason repented the insane and angry spate of words that tumbled out. She accused him of everything she could think of.

'Men like you—you ought to be locked up! Uncle Ed was right about your family, they can't be trusted, so you can take you rotten ideas somewhere else. You planned something like this from the beginning, didn't you? You and your separate tents! But you can forget whatever you had in mind. I'd rather drown out there.'

Appalled, Danni listened to the angry words tumbling out in what she recognised as the verge of hysteria. She went on fumbling with the door-handle as he bit out levelly,

'Are you finished?' The anger in his face was as hard as granite. 'Sure there's nothing else you want to scream at me? Don't you have some other insults stored up in that rubbish bin you call a brain?'

He took a step towards her and she panted, still out of control, 'Touch me, and I'll cry rape.'

'I'm sure you will, and you'll make sure somebody hears you too, I'll bet. That's the whole idea, isn't it?'

He strode across the room and stood beside her, looking down in rage, eyes glittering as if he wished his anger were made of steel and he could cut her down with it.

'For your information, Miss Danielle Paige, I did not plan this storm. It's a damned nuisance and so are you. I should have known better than to bring a blasted unpredictable female with me, and a member of the Paige family at that.'

He grabbed her arm and when she recoiled and jerked away he shot out both arms and spun her around until her body was jammed hard against his own.

'Let's get this little matter settled once for all. I'm not going to have you breathing outrage down my neck for the next two weeks, going over the top every time I look your way, and screeching your head off like a shrew.' He tightened his grasp. 'I don't want you. I don't think you're all that desirable. I can't imagine what bloody idiot gave you the notion you set a man on fire every time he looks at you.' Brutally, he pushed her away. 'Now get back into bed. We'll sort this out in the morning.'

'No.' The atmosphere was stifling her. She had nowhere to go. Outside the thunder and the lightning waited with malevolence. Inside, she had this claustrophobic sensation, as if all the fresh air had been drained away and she couldn't breathe. Heavy rain rattled on the tin roof in drumbeats that her tension magnified, so that they echoed in her head. Everywhere was menace, and it all had to be in her imagination, but she couldn't deal with it.

'I can't stay here,' she gasped. 'Not with you! I don't know what my family is supposed to have done to your father and I don't care. I bet he deserved it and you do too—you—you devil——'

She had no more words. Uncle Edwin's troubled face swam in front of her blurring eyes and she blinked it away fiercely, but it seemed to take the last of her strength.

'Hell!' The dark man watched her swaying, then once again cupped his hands over her shoulders, fingers biting into flesh, and when she offered no resistance he began to shake her. He wasn't bothering about charisma now. He was angry, and it took all her will-power to mumble,

'I told you. I'll cry rape,' and he stiffened, thrusting his furious face close to hers, his hands stilled.

'Yes. Of course you will. That's the whole purpose of this little scene, isn't it?' Contempt glittered in his eyes. 'Did you set me up, Danni, sitting there with the light shining on your hair?'

The soft chilling voice sent little currents of fear stirring on her skin.

She said, 'Oh lord! Of course it wasn't,' but he didn't listen.

'You certainly took a lot of trouble to stage the scene, didn't you?' His lips curled. 'All that shining brushed hair falling on to your shoulders and that innocent look—big green eyes wide. And what's the perfume, Danni?' He sniffed, lips tight, eyes glacial. 'Very delicate, quite fragrant. So there you sat under the light, pretending to read, playing the seductive witch—or should it be bitch? Gave your hair some extra brushing, didn't you?' His scathing glance swept her from head to toe. 'And that cute cotton nightshirt—that's a smart move. How did you find out that can be just as much a turn-on as satin and lace? You weren't far wrong. Something to do with the piquant touch——'

Danni protested through stiff lips, 'No,' but he didn't listen.

'Oh yes, you're a clever girl, Danni, but I doubt whether you're quite smart enough. Let's find out, shall we?'

Once again he curved those implacable hands over her shoulders, cupping them in strong fingers, staring down at her out of hatefully impersonal eyes.

'Come a little closer,' he ordered softly, and when Danni stood her ground the fingers again bit in more tightly, pressing her towards him. Then he bent his head and trapped her lips with his own, showing no gentleness at all. It was a mockery of a kissing, she endured it

without struggling, instinct telling her that might in-
flame his anger even further.

When he lifted his head he glowered down at her
cynically.

'Not exactly earth-shaking,' he commented.

Danni moistened her dry and swollen lips with the tip
of her tongue and saw instantly that this was the wrong
thing to do. He thought it provocative, and gave a short
hard laugh before he bent his head and clamped his own
mouth hard over hers again. He meant to continue the
punishment, and this was a meanly punishing gesture.
Danni winced as she felt her wide soft mouth forced
open by his bitter assault. He amused himself with revenge, she thought, and with a frantic movement brought
her knee up and thrust forward blindly.

It didn't work, she should have known he would be
too strong for her. But it did interrupt the kissing. He
lifted his head, eyebrows arched derisively, and Danni
waited with foreboding for what was going to happen
next.

She expected him to claim her lips again; instead he
grasped both her wrists in one strong hand and pinioned
her arms behind her back, then with his free arm he
reached out and slowly, deliberately, began to unbutton
the front of the white cotton nightshirt, easing it down
from one shoulder, then the other, with strong hard
fingers, until finally the crisp white cotton, urged by his
fingers, dropped to reveal her breasts. He bent down
and teased with his lips first one, then the other, and
Danni stood yielding, trapped by her own responses, because even in anger this man was powerful beyond anything she had ever known.

He moved her imprisoned hands from behind her own
back and placed them, palms open, against his chest,
and the roughness and texture of the dark curls under
her fingers made Danni's senses lurch.

Under her right hand she felt the strong and steady beating of his heart, and she could not have pulled that hand away if her whole future had depended on it.

He held her there, secured by some kind of dynamic currents of sensation that swept her away on a pleasure-flight of feeling more intense than anything she had ever before experienced.

He moved her slightly away from him so that he could use his hands over her body to stir up new feelings, his skin touching her skin, setting it on fire in the tingling language of sensuality.

She felt warm skin and roughened fingertips as he trailed his outspread hands from her waist to her thighs, all the time watching her from his greater height, accepting her responses, delighting in them.

Then suddenly his own body trembled and he clutched her suddenly close. She felt his mouth against her slender throat, pressed against sensitive skin, feathering her throat and shoulders with kisses, lightly at first, then growing in intensity.

And somewhere in the core of herself—her real self—Danni felt an ecstatic rush of incredible pleasure that left her without inhibition, so that she curved her body impulsively against his, reaching up to twist her arms protectively, invitingly, around his strong shoulders and pull his head towards her. The skin of his cheek was warm and damp under her mouth and again the faint trembling shook him, as he lifted his head, twisted strong fingers in her hair, uptilted her face and guided her mouth to his.

Danni didn't need to be an expert to know she was into something deeper than she could handle. His lips were teasing, provoking hers gently but implacably, the warmth of his body revitalising her. This time it wasn't an assault; more like an infusion of awareness that swept over her body until her whole skin tingled.

Danni became pliant, then passionate, making small desperate noises in her throat as she touched him, wanting him, abandoned to everything but the desire to be part of Jay's world—part of Jay.

Then just as she waited for the final wave of feeling to sweep them away towards the magnificent climax, it all ended. Jay pulled himself deliberately away from her needing hands.

'Enough, I think.'

She stared at him dumbly. Something in his eyes sent chills feathering across the heat of her feeling. He hesitated.

'Do you want me, Danni?' and she nodded.

He picked her up and strode with her to the bed, putting her down none too gently. She waited for him to make a move, any kind of move, that suggested he wanted to lie there with her, but it was the face of a cool, detached stranger that looked down at her. The reflection from the lamp over her bed hardened the contours of his face. His voice was cool.

'Don't you want to scream?' he taunted. 'Not that I think anybody will hear you now, in all this rain and thunder. What a shame. You could have created quite a disturbance.'

And when she did not—could not—answer, he went on,

'You understand, Miss Danielle Paige, I could have done whatever I wanted with you?'

Helplessly, Danni nodded.

'And I didn't. So that should answer all those frantic accusations.'

Danni clutched at the last of her pride. 'I gather you were amusing yourself.'

'No. I was making a point.'

She said icily, 'And the point is——'

'The point is that I could have taken you and I didn't. I won't say you aren't desirable. I grant you have, shall we say, certain possibilities. But you are not irresistible, and I do not rape, and if I hear that word again I'll shake you until your teeth rattle.' Relentless arms pinned her down on to the pillow. 'So I'll have an apology. I think one is overdue, don't you?'

Of course he was right. She had been completely carried away, his for the taking. And he hadn't taken.

Embarrassment coloured Danni's face. 'OK. You can have your apology. I'm sorry I shrieked at you, I don't know what happened to me. I don't usually go overboard.'

'Good. We'll get on fine so long as you register the fact that I'm not even vaguely interested in your body. It's an efficient assistant I need right now.' He took his hands away from her shoulders. 'So now we understand each other.'

The words were spoken flatly, not slanted as a question, but he obviously expected—no, demanded— an answer, as he stood glaring down at her implacably, and Danni mumbled, 'Yes.'

'And the next time you decide to be provocative, lady—think carefully.'

He turned and padded barefoot across the carpet to his divan. Danni reached up and turned off the light. Understand him! She would never understand him in a million years.

She let her head drop back on to the pillow. She had no energy left, it was all drained away by the icy douche of cold water his last few words had delivered. So much for pride . . . he wasn't even vaguely interested.

She must have imagined the ardour, fooled herself about the need that set his hips moving against her own, the urgent heat of his mouth on her skin.

Not even vaguely interested, she reminded herself bitterly. She ought to be grateful. And of course she was.

She lay in bed, listening to the rain. Oh, Jackson North had chalked himself up a victory, all right. Danni cringed inwardly as she lay in bed, staring up at the dark ceiling, quite sure she would never sleep.

Danni had always liked pleasant sensations, but this was her first encounter with a man who could set a woman on fire. His expert arousal had made her wanton, craving the fulfilment of everything his warm hands and hard muscles, the hot skin of his body, had promised her. He could have had anything he wanted and he had wanted nothing, apart from the knowledge that he could do what he liked with her.

Those breathless, broken cries she had uttered must surely have told him there was nothing she would not surrender if he asked for it. But he could take her or leave her, and wasn't that just what he had done?

Danni tried to tell herself that perhaps it was the crazy mixed-up state of her emotions that had made her so defenceless. It must have been that. In her right mind she would never have responded.

Another time, surely, she would be able to handle the situation more coolly... but how could she be sure?

CHAPTER FIVE

THE world had changed when Danni woke up next morning. It was not yet daylight, but there was no rain drumming on the roof, no grumble of thunder, and the sound of the shower running told her Jay was already up and about.

She slid quickly out of bed, not anxious to have him around while she dressed.

He came out of the bathroom dressed in light cotton shorts and casual black and white striped polo top, rubbing his damp hair with a towel, glancing at Danni with eyes that were cool and impersonal.

'Breakfast in fifteen minutes. Better eat a hearty meal, you're only getting sandwiches for lunch.'

He was pretending last night had never happened, and that was all right with Danni. She breathed a sigh of relief.

She washed and dressed while Jay gathered up equipment, and she boosted her morale—she hoped—by wearing the white shirt with its saucy painted crab over a pair of denim jeans, and when she came out Jay raised an eyebrow but the only thing he said was, 'We have to cover a lot of territory today. I'd like to get away in a hurry.'

The girl from the café arrived with two breakfast trays and a large packet of sandwiches and buns, a thermos of tea and some cans of lemonade that Jay stowed in the portable car fridge.

After breakfast he waited while Danni made a quick check to make sure they had left nothing behind, then he whistled for Lionel, and they were on their way.

As they drove through the gateway they passed a large semi-trailer and a small green jeep parked alongside a row of gum trees on their side of the run-off. Apart from that the world could have been uninhabited except for a flock of white cockatoos, a pair of kookaburras and the high dark shape of an eagle gliding in a thermal current high overhead.

As they drove Jay asked casually, 'How are you on handling cameras?'

'Nothing marvellous,' Danni admitted honestly. 'I've had some experience with a still camera, just the usual hobby stuff, but I know absolutely nothing about taking movies.'

'OK.' The two cameras lay between them on the front seat. He nodded towards the smaller. 'Familiarise yourself with the thirty-five-millimetre job. It's not complicated. We'll keep both handy, you never know when something will flash into view that makes a good shot. Everything moves very quickly, and you'll have to learn to snap to it as soon as I pull up, or even sooner. Keep alert and make a noise if you see anything highly dramatic or unusual.'

Danni thought privately that it didn't look as if anything dramatic or unusual ever happened here. The countryside around them was fairly flat, occasional stretches of bushland but mostly grassy paddocks where sheep or cattle browsed among scattered gnarled eucalypts. Then gradually the country around them changed mood and shape.

The scenery became repetitive, empty spaces stretching to the horizon with occasional heaps of red and orange rocks and gnarled and twisted gum trees brooding among grasses more brown than green. Sometimes, a line of jagged mountains would stand harshly against the sky in the distance. Compared with the coastal scenery it could have been a landscape from another planet.

There were occasional puffs of dust as scattered cattle moved dejectedly, or a lazy eddy of wind stirred the red earth in the heat, then collapsed as if quickly deprived of energy.

Danni realised why Jay wore light clothing. The heat didn't affect him at all, he stayed cool and comfortable while she sweltered, and she leaned down and rolled up the denim jeans, kicking off her shoes.

As they drove steadily west and north-west Danni stole a look at the man beside her. It seemed incredible that last night she would have given him anything he asked. This morning he was coolly casual, even remote. He had lit all the fires he wanted; now he was letting them die down.

She set about studying the camera with a kind of desperate intensity that gradually simmered down into genuine interest.

It was a very good camera, an expensive model. Danni didn't know a great deal about cameras but she did know about this one, that it was worth far more money than the casual but effective cameras she was used to.

Some months ago a friend had suggested she write a few nature articles for a magazine. She had experimented with a fairly good still camera and she was thankful for that now. She had a feeling Jackson North would not tolerate fumbling.

Of course she did not know how to handle the extra lenses and filters stacked in the carrier bags but at least she had a fair idea of composition, and she could do what she was told. She hoped that would be enough.

When she put down the camera North said, 'That one of your creations you're wearing?' He meant the crab and Danni said half apologetically, 'Not one of my top efforts, but I took a fancy to it.'

He grinned at that. 'I must say it has a certain panache.' He let a few seconds pass before he asked, 'How much writing have you done?' It sounded a genuine question but he could have been trying to find out how experienced she was. Danni gave it some thought before she answered evasively, 'I think I was born with the urge. I've had it ever since I can remember. When I was a precocious little girl I used to write plays for the other kids to act in our back yard. I always wanted to write. My father——'

She stopped. Mention of her father's name had brought a fierce and frightening reaction out on North's island, but this time Jay pressed softly, 'Yes? Go on,' without showing any emotion at all.

Danni bit her lower lip and went on doggedly, 'My father was a journalist.'

That surprised him. He gave her a quick sharp glance, the grey eyes probing.

'I didn't know that. Tell me more.'

'Nothing fancy. He worked as a police roundsman and did the usual reporting jobs on a newspaper. That was before he—before he and Uncle Edwin went digging for opals——'

Danni didn't want to talk about that. It was an explosive subject. Her tongue shied away definitely from discussing the opal diggings with this man.

And she had misled Jackson North about the extent of her father's work as a journalist. He had been offered promotion, a daily column with his own byline, just as he and Edwin were preparing to leave for the outback. Lilyan Paige had sighed faintly as she told Danni and Gregg about that.

Ryan Paige had chosen to keep his promise to go digging for opals with his brother and Gardiner North, but Danni had the impression it was out of loyalty to Edwin and perhaps not the decision he would have preferred to make. He had his chance to become a columnist, just what he had always hoped for, and he had to turn it down to chase elusive opals and resign his newspaper job altogether.

But Danni couldn't tell that to the man sitting beside her. Thinking about opals reminded her of the opal jewellery and the disturbing possibility that the North family might have stolen it. Maybe he was pumping her for information, trying to find out how much she knew. So perhaps it was time she asked a few questions herself.

Danni sat up straight in her seat. 'What are you going to do after you finish this documentary?'

He raised cool eyebrows. 'I really haven't decided. There are a couple of options in the melting-pot. I'll sort them out when I get this baby out of the way.'

'Do you plan to write books some day, or will you always stick to filming? Do you ever think of branching out into other fields?'

'You ask a lot of questions.' He didn't approve.

Danni said pertly, 'I might want to write an interview or an article about you some day, and this is my big chance, isn't it? The famous Jackson North seen close up.'

'Don't try it. I'll sue you.' His lips tightened to grimness. 'You're here to work as my assistant, not to boost your own career—such as it is.'

The cheek of the man! Danni sat fuming beside him. She certainly wasn't going to ask him anything else, and they drove in silence along the red road until he said mildly, 'By the way, you didn't answer my question yesterday,' and when she remained stubbornly silent he added, 'About your future.'

'You mean, it's all right for you to ask me questions?'

'That's right. I'm your boss.'

'Well, I don't think my future is any concern of yours except that I expect you to keep your word and leave our caravan park alone.'

'Is Derek a vital part of your future plans?'

'How should I know? You'll have to ask him.'

She didn't know exactly why she reacted so swiftly at the suggestion. She and Derek certainly had a—what was it?—not a relationship as yet. A blossoming friendship perhaps, likely to develop into what?

She said abruptly, 'I haven't sat down at my desk and plotted things out. Perhaps I'm not very ambitious.' She might have added, I was happy with the life I was living until you came along, but she didn't, because that would have sounded defensive.

She shrugged her shoulders and the man beside her laughed, a real laugh that dispersed the grimness from his features and added a new and somehow disturbing dimension, an attraction she hadn't expected ever to see on those harsh features, not in her direction, anyway.

'For a highly spirited female you seem to have been lax about organising your future.' He returned his attention to the driving. 'Never mind. Hold the camera on your lap and make sure your seat-belt is fastened firmly. The road gets bumpier from now on.'

The road certainly did get rougher. Danni was glad to stretch her legs when they finally stopped for lunch. Way out in the middle of nowhere Jay had turned and headed for a small tree-surrounded pool covered with the mauve flowers of wild iris.

They ate in shade beside the trees while Lionel chased first a lizard then a dragonfly, capturing neither, although Jay made Danni take several photographs. For sentiment only, he said, and to learn how to use the camera; but when a flock of small green budgerigars, noisy and agitated, fluttered down to settle in a tree, he took the camera himself.

Danni watched, fascinated despite herself, as he stalked the birds, moving lithely, intently, on swift sure feet as he took his pictures.

After a few restless flutterings they seemed to accept him. Once or twice a few of them moved uneasily and Jay froze. Danni knew all his concentration was on the job he was doing, and the dog Lionel, well trained, watched quietly from under the vehicle.

When he finished his picture-taking Jay turned to the dog. 'OK. Stir them up,' he ordered and Lionel, barking joyfully, hurtled towards the gum tree, sending a cloud of indignant green birds billowing into the air.

Jay snapped several more pictures of the swirling flock before handing the camera to Danni.

'Got your notebook?' He read her the numbers of the film exposures, the location, date and other information he might want to use later.

'Probably not worth anything, but they might come in handy for publicity shots.'

He settled beside her, munching a buttered bun, and the glance he gave her flushed cheeks was keen.

'I hope you aren't going to wilt in the heat.'

It sounded a fairly innocent comment but Danni knew he was watching her carefully. She was feeling breathless, a little dizzy, and her cheeks were undeniably warm. If she wilted in this heat she could become an encumbrance when they got into really barren country.

'I can take it,' she snapped resentfully. 'Don't waste your time waiting for me to melt before we get where we're going.'

He grinned. 'That could be taken two ways,' he murmured provocatively, but Danni closed her eyes. He was too quick-witted, too fast on the innuendo. She couldn't afford to spend time crossing verbal swords with him.

She poured mugs of tea and when they were empty Jay said with what sounded like reluctance, 'I suppose we'd better be on our way.'

Danni looked at him quickly, and to her astonishment a faint smile crinkled the corners of his mouth.

'I feel a great temptation to fall asleep in the midday sun,' he admitted wryly. 'It often happens to me, especially if I didn't sleep the sleep of the innocent the night before,' and Danni found herself almost softening, almost smiling back at him, until she remembered this was Jay North and you didn't take too much of what he said at face-value. So his remark might or might not have been by way of apology but Danni wasn't taking any chances.

They had left the trees and the pool and the birds, and were turning on to the dusty road again, when they saw the green four-wheel-drive parked discreetly behind the clustered trunks of several dry old trees. It was not really concealed, there wasn't enough growing along the roadside to screen it completely, but it was the nearest its driver could have got to a hiding-place, and Danni saw Jay's forehead pleat suddenly into hard creases as he noticed it there.

He said nothing, did nothing, until they had travelled some distance along the road, then as they approached an enormous jagged orange rock on the roadside Jay put his foot down hard on the brake and swerved sharply. Their vehicle stopped with a grinding jerk, so close to the boulder Danni thought they were going to hit it. She flinched, shrinking closer to the driver, then moved away quickly.

Jay was angry, with a powerful anger that vibrated around them.

Danni had noticed him watching in the rear-view mirror, and once had even dared turn her own head to see the puff of dust that told her the smaller vehicle was travelling behind them still, though at a discreet distance.

They stayed hidden behind the rocks as the other vehicle drew nearer, hearing the sound of its motor, and then at last it passed. Puffs of dust churned and small particles flew off the road surface and pattered against the Range Rover. The other vehicle passed noisily and disappeared from view.

Jay glowered at Danni. 'All right, lady,' he bit out. 'Who do you know owns a green four-wheel-drive?' and Danni stared at him, confused.

'Nobody. I don't know anyone who owns anything like that.'

'All right. Somebody who might have hired one?'

Jay's face was hot and unyielding, the anger showing through. Hard lines deepened on the tanned cheeks and jawbone, and his eyes glittered. There was a vibrance about his burst of fury that intimidated, but Danni steeled herself.

'Look, that green thing is nothing to do with me. I don't know what you're talking about. Don't you accuse me——'

Jay's fingers remained clenched on the steering-wheel, then he deliberately loosened them, curving the fingers, letting go, his anger more controlled as he turned towards her.

'Listen, if you and your damn-fool family have cooked up some cockeyed plan to have us followed, forget it. It won't work. I'll ditch anybody who trails me. I know this country and I can take care of any threats. If I get mad enough I'll lead whoever is on our tail to a place he'll never get out of, nor his damned transport either. I'll see he finishes up at the bottom of the biggest hole I can find.'

He shot out a hand and gripped Danni's chin and jerked her face close to his. She gasped, twisting away.

'Stop it. You're hurting me.'

'I meant to.'

Jay's face was bent so close to hers she could feel the heat of his breath, see the dust flecks on his skin.

'Tell me, Danni, just exactly who is that idiot trying to follow us?'

For some reason the extent and force of Jay's anger brought back balance to Danni. He was really fussed, cool, calm Jay North who never let anything shake him out of control, and in some perverse way Danni felt it could be something of a victory.

As if he tuned in to her thinking Jay loosened his fingers and pushed her away from him.

'I hope it's not that fool of a young brother of yours. If it is, he won't last a week out here, so you'd better tell me——'

'Don't be ridiculous.'

'Has he any experience driving in this kind of country?'

'No.'

'Hmm.' His anger was simmering down. 'How about Derek?'

'That's even more ridiculous.'

The betraying words were out before she could stop them and Danni squirmed. She caught the gleam of irony in Jay's sharp eyes.

'Not the heroic type, hmm?' That seemed to put him in a better humour. 'You seem very sure of that.'

He was deliberately letting her know he picked up the vibes in that giveaway remark that admitted so promptly how unlikely it was that Derek would abandon his gallery and his mother to trek around the countryside, worried for her safety.

Jay added another gibe as he put their four-wheel-drive in gear and moved back on to the road.

'It certainly wouldn't be your dear old Uncle Edwin, would it?'

'I don't know what you're talking about.' He gave a short hard laugh and Danni sat stiffly beside him as they surged forward, but of course she did know what he meant by that acid comment. He was pointing out that her uncle wasn't likely to be valiant either, that she didn't have any heroes likely to abandon their own interests and come stampeding after them to protect her, and somehow that diminished her pride.

·She sat crumpled in her seat, feeling unaccountably depressed, because in that instantaneous quick denial about Derek she had somehow lost a fantasy that could have been very sweet and satisfying. Derek wasn't chasing after her; he was probably sitting at home in his gallery, sulking, and that made her feel sad. Perhaps she had cared more about Derek than she realised.

She sat staring at the red road ahead, finally closing her eyes against the heat and the glare, until what seemed a weary while later she felt the four-wheel-drive slowing down and turning off the road, and Jay opened his door and got out to open a gate.

As he climbed back into his seat he said crisply, 'That's your job from now on. You can open the gates, so you'd better start sitting up and taking notice.'

Danni said crossly, 'I'll open the next one. Better still, I'll get out and shut this gate after us when we're through,' and Jay said, 'That's better.'

Once again Danni had the eerie feeling that he had somehow plugged in to her train of thought and understood the faintly bitter taste of the instant truth she had just handed herself.

They crawled along beside the banks of a dry river-bed, Jay explaining why he was not driving along the leveller surface of the dry bed itself, although it could have been easier travelling.

'Very deceiving country, this. It can be dry and hot as hell in one place, and suddenly this wall of water will come belting along the dry river-bed and sweep you away, all because it rained somewhere a hundred miles away. So I'm afraid you'll have to put up with some lurching and bumping until we get where we're going.'

'And where are we going?'

'This is where we'll find my Aboriginal friend, the man with the tumour on his leg. We're going to find out how he's progressing. He's an elder in the tribe that has land rights over this area and runs it as a cattle station and craft centre.

'They carve boomerangs and other wooden weapons and decorate them, they paint pictures and symbols on bark, and a couple of the young fellows paint emu eggs. You're free to buy anything that takes your fancy, although most of it is marketed elsewhere, and our main project here is to interview Tomi Ollerah. We shan't have time for much else.'

He went on, 'Our film shows him explaining his philosophy, including his unshakeable belief that there are many ways to heal, not all of them in the medical books. I hope he's not mistaken.' He gave her a quizzical look. 'I think you'll find him interesting.'

'I hope his tribal magic is working, if that's what it is.'

Jay smiled quietly. 'It doesn't matter all that much to him. There are other things more important to a wise man than the number of days he lives. That's what Tomi says, anyway. He's a grand old man and I'm looking forward to meeting him again.'

They moved on to a meandering line of dusty wheel-tracks on the red earth and Danni asked no more questions. Eventually they drove to the foot of a high and much eroded wall of rock, almost completely barren, more desolate than anything Danni had ever seen, and she was thankful when they left it behind them, turned at right angles and headed towards a cluster of buildings.

A group of Aboriginal children ran towards them, chattering and cheering. This was Jay's welcome. They clustered around the stationary vehicle, calling his name, exclaiming excitedly as he reached into the rear of the vehicle and handed them presents. He had come well prepared.

The children escorted Jay and Danni towards the largest building, including Danni in their welcome as if they had known her for much longer than just a few minutes, and she was taken to see the artists painting on bark stripped from the trees, drawing intricate symbols in white and red, orange and ochre and black. Fascinated, Danni would have lingered, but Jay guided her away, though not before she was allowed to purchase a large emu egg covered in intriguing patterns, which Jay stowed away in the Range Rover.

Lionel enjoyed himself frisking with the large and varied collection of dogs that lounged around the settlement.

But it was Tomi Ollerah that Jay had come to visit, and he sat quietly apart on the veranda of one of the smaller houses. His deep brown eyes stared at Danni out of a dark face creased into countless wrinkles, the marks of old age, experience and wisdom. His hair and beard were tinged with grey but the smile that flashed when Jay introduced Danni was vibrant and full of good humour.

Danni sat silent, letting Jay ask his questions. Tomi was not disturbed by the tape recorder or the camera. He accepted both with mild good nature, grey-white eyebrows rising and falling in gestures of exaggerated mockery, as if he considered it odd that the younger man in the prime of his strength should require a memory-jogger to record the conversation. He answered Jay's questions in a deep, melodious voice.

'All gone,' he announced, pointing to the leg which had carried the tumour and now looked just like the other. He nodded at Jay with obvious satisfaction. 'Lump all gone. That fellow cancer, I sing him away.'

'Are you sure about that, Tomi?'

'Oh sure.' The old man nodded again, this time even more vigorously. 'I have faith in my spirits and the spirits of my tribe, and the bad creature in my body him all gone—finished. I sing him away—like this.'

He began to chant, a low rise and fall of sound meaningless to Danni. Oblivious to the tape recorder he sang softly, his eyes became introspective, his thoughts turned inward. When the chanting finished he said dreamily, 'My good spirit, the spirit of my people, he take care of me. The bad thing in my leg, him all gone away now.' He touched his leg with an old gnarled hand. 'I walk now, all right.' His delighted grin embraced them. 'I walk fine. I whole feller now. The bad one inside me, him all sung away.'

His eyes stayed reflective, brown pupils gleaming under wrinkled lids. A strange tranquillity seemed to have entered the veranda where they sat.

They talked a little longer and with Tomi's permission Jay took several pictures, before the afternoon wind sprang up and the dry grass moved restlessly.

When they made their farewells and drove away Danni felt she could have visited another country, so unfamiliar did everything seem.

They moved off in another chorus of friendly shouts from the children, but as they approached the towering rock wall Jay gave an exclamation.

'Damn. Looks like a willy-willy coming our way. It could peter out before it reaches us but we won't take any chances.'

He swung the four-wheel-drive into the shelter of the rocks, crawling over the uneven surface until they reached the far end, where he pulled up near a sheltering overhang. 'Think I'll get some pictures. Would you like to watch?'

'Yes, please.'

'There's a cave up in the rock. It might be a good viewpoint.'

Jay closed the windows of the Range Rover, tucked Lionel under one arm and handed the still camera to Danni, waiting until she secured the long strap over her shoulder. The dog huddled secure and silent, as if he understood this was not a moment for play, and Jay signed for Danni to climb ahead of him through a narrow ascending cleft in the rock that widened into a cave at the top.

They crouched quietly, watching the spiralling chimney of sand twist and sway as it moved over the land towards them. Sticks and leaves and fragments of bark corkscrewed in a rising-falling motion, as the willy-willy swung towards them.

As it came closer to the rocks it veered away towards a clump of spindly trees, filling the air with the swishing sound of rustling leaves and dry grass.

Lionel perched beside Jay, apparently unperturbed by the eerie column of spinning sand, and Danni thought how strange it was that such a disturbing man as Jay could provide so great a feeling of security.

Jay had taken the camera and secured several pictures. Then he turned his attention to the walls of the cave on which there were several rather simple-looking pictures painted. They were mostly paintings of hands, with fingers outspread, and others of gradually widening circles, like ripples spreading on water.

Danni asked uneasily, 'Is this a sacred place?' but Jay shook his head.

'There are sacred places hidden deep in these rocks, places of initiation, fertility and other rites, but this is not one of them. If it were, we wouldn't be here. Those hand paintings are just what they look like, made by holding the hand with fingers outspread against the rock and painting around it.

'And the spirals, are they willy-willies?'

Jay shook his head. 'No. They are records of hunting trips. The hunting is done in circles, each day a farther distance from the central camp.'

Here in the cave, high above the land, Jackson North had become almost approachable, and Danni ventured a question.

'Is the old man's—Tomi's—cancer really cured?'

'It certainly looks that way. If you'd seen his leg eighteen months ago you wouldn't have given him a chance.'

'Do you believe he really did "sing it away" like he says?'

'Who knows? Nobody knows.' He glanced at her obliquely. He was not going to tell her what he felt, and Danni pressed,

'Tomi had therapy in hospital?'

'Yes. Then he came back to commune with the spirits of his tribe, and with his own personal "spirit". You could call it a form of meditation if you like, or a way of calling on forces outside the ordinary civilised man's comprehension, whichever you feel like doing.'

'I see. So you wouldn't know for sure exactly what cured his malignancy, or even if it's permanently cured, although it certainly looks normal.'

'No. Nobody could say for sure.' He didn't look directly at her as he answered. There was distance in his eyes, a remoteness about his expression.

He stared sombrely down over the land below, at the dry grass and the scattered trees, and where the willy-willy had passed and spent itself in the group of spindly

trees there was now an uneasy silence, as if the torn-off
leaves and scattered debris waited to be lifted again and
thrown about and borne away, as if they could not settle
where they lay. But nothing happened. The whirling
column of sand was history.

'I'm glad Tomi's had his miracle, however it happened.' Jay looked squarely at Danni. 'I wouldn't like
to guess what brought about the magic. Let's leave it a
question, shall we?'

'But you believe he might have sung it away, as he
claims?'

Jay shrugged. 'Who can say? Maybe the cure, or the
remission, whichever it is—maybe the change was
brought about by a combination of many things. No
doubt tribal man has a communication with nature that
so-called civilised men don't understand. Perhaps he can
plug in to some force or power the white man lost gen-
erations ago. Who knows? I suppose we could have lost
a lot of things.'

But not you, Danni thought. You haven't lost it. She
almost spoke the words aloud, she was so sure. She
glanced furtively at the sun-tanned form crouched now
beside her with knees bent so that his long strong arms
could reach the pebbles on the floor of the cave.

He fingered an odd-shaped piece of brown stone, a
conglomerate with strange white markings, turning it
between his sun-tanned fingers as if absorbing the
texture—as if, Danni thought with sudden insight, as if
it were a living thing that could speak to him.

And suddenly she felt an intruder, a stranger, shut out
from whatever Jay was experiencing as he rolled the piece
of stone in his hands. She felt lonely, even afraid. She
had no way of knowing whether the people who had left
those symbols on the wall of the cave were people of
today, or many yesterdays ago, but she knew that

whoever they were Jay had something in common with them.

He understood their dreaming, and the strange and powerful communication they had with nature.

She shivered, and Jay dropped the stone and stood up, taking her arm and leading her to the edge of the cave.

'Show is over,' he said. 'Time for us to leave.'

He collected Lionel and they scrambled down to the Range Rover, and stowed the camera away.

Slyly Danni watched Jay's hands on the wheel as they drove across the red dust and dry grass, trying not to remember the eeriness of those moments in the cave; and once he turned and raised his eyebrows, tilting his mouth into a wry shape, as if he guessed she had been thrown a little off balance by the events of the afternoon.

Danni was tired. She could have closed her eyes against the monotonous landscape and the sound of the motor throbbing.

Later she was to wish that she had done just that, because when they reached the gate on the boundary of the property, and she got out ready to open it for Jay to drive through, Danni glanced up and down the red dirt road and her heart lurched, because she saw the small green four-wheel-drive waiting between two spreading gum trees in the distance behind them.

CHAPTER SIX

JAY made no comment as Danni got back into her seat
after shutting the gate securely behind them, but Danni
knew he had seen the unobtrusive small green vehicle
parked so discreetly in the distance, waiting for them to
come back to the road.

With misgivings she watched the sensuous lips tighten
until they became taut and angry, a hard line that
augured ill for somebody. His whole body seemed to
tense, like an animal in a threatened situation, and Danni
decided heaven help the driver if Jay let his temper loose.
She huddled in her corner, imagination flashing her a
vivid picture of Jay dragging the other driver from his
seat and beating him into the red dust.

He could do it without any trouble, spurred on by the
anger that vibrated in the Range Rover, sending shock-
waves even to the rear where Lionel moved restlessly and
whimpered, looking at Danni with distressed, questioning eyes when she turned to look at him.

She huddled back in her seat. Suppose, just suppose,
it really was Gregg back there, her foolish young brother.
Oh lord, no, Danni prayed silently, surely it couldn't be;
Gregg would never venture into the unknown outback,
not until he had a little more experience anyway. He was
a level-headed youth.

And once again every instinct told Danni that it was
not likely to be Derek, leaving his mother and his
precious gallery to come streaking after her. Derek was
not protective of her. Of himself, maybe, or his material
possessions; and he was probably very fond of her in his

own way—he certainly acted that way—but common sense told Danni he was unlikely to come dashing across the countryside to rescue her from threat.

Danni faced it squarely, sitting with the taciturn man beside her: what she and Derek felt for each other was a mixture of mild affection and the fact that they were useful to each other.

She had been impressed and flattered when Fiona's brother sought her out. Who wouldn't be? A well known local artist and gallery-owner, good-looking and sought after, and good-natured too. She had always complemented him well as a companion, always been willing to do what he asked, go where he wished, finding it easy to please him and comfortable to be beside him. But of course, she saw now, there had to be much more to a relationship than that if it was ever going to set the world, or themselves, on fire.

She must have sighed aloud. Jay gave her a quick look, relaxed a little, settled himself more comfortably behind the wheel.

'Cheer up, Danielle. I can only flatten him against a tree or beat his head off.'

'Very sure of yourself, aren't you?'

'I am.' He really was incredibly arrogant.

'Don't forget what they say—pride goes before a tumble.'

'So long as you tumble with me.'

'I've no intention of doing anything with you that is not strictly business.'

He shifted in his seat, his leg brushing against hers as he stretched, and it took all Danni's will-power not to pull away.

'Careful, Danni,' he goaded. 'I might regard that last remark as a challenge.'

'In that case you'll have to flatten *me* against a tree.'

His glance was oblique. To Danni's surprise a smile played softly around the corners of his mouth.

'That wasn't exactly what I had in mind but I dare say it would make a good start, and if you keep provoking me maybe that's just what I'll do.'

Danni was careful not to look back to check whether the other driver still followed behind them. If he was there she didn't want to know.

They refuelled at an isolated settlement consisting of a couple of ancient houses, a line of boab trees with bulging trunks, and a weather-beaten pub and store with a petrol pump outside.

Still Danni dared not look back, but Jay's expression had resumed its grimness, so she guessed the small four-wheel-drive still hovered behind them somewhere on their trail.

Jay climbed down to fill up with fuel and he said, 'I'll book us in for a quick drink, a shower and brush-up, if you feel like it, but we have to push on quickly. We won't have time yet to stop for a meal. We'll eat when we get where we're going.'

Danni changed into a fresh lime-coloured sun-dress after freshening up, it made her feel slim and cool, and the drink Jay offered was just what she needed.

When they came outside he pointed to the driver's seat. 'Your turn. You may as well keep your hand in.'

She reached for sunglasses as Jay settled back to check his script and make notes.

It was almost sunset when she turned off the road under Jay's instructions and pulled up beside a riverbed which was now no more than a chain of shallow waterholes separated by bars of rock and sand. Birds were already arriving for the evening. They made a great fuss around the waterholes as Jay set up camp, pitching the two small tents under a tree. He plugged the car fridge into the battery and helped Danni select meat for the gas barbecue.

The shadowing green vehicle was nowhere to be seen, and for that Danni was profoundly thankful.

While the meal cooked Jay set up a folding table and dictated while Danni typed, and they ate not long afterwards in the brightness of sunset. The flames of afterglow flung scarlet shapes across the sky when Danni went to the nearest waterhole to wash dishes. She would not be sorry to retire into her tent; this had been a trying day, and not even the brilliance around her could soothe away the uneasy feelings she carried with her, though it certainly helped.

She was standing beside the water, looking up at the sky, when Jay joined her.

'I took a couple of quick pictures, hope you don't mind, but you look quite dramatic silhouetted against that sky. Like the trees, except——' his lips quirked '—a lot more shapely and seductive.'

'I've been doing my job—washing the dishes.'

'Yes.' The smiling vanished from his face. 'And I wonder if you know what else you've been doing, standing there and casting your spells on the evening. You can cast spells, Danni, can't you? And I expect you know it.'

The face was stern now, reserved and unsmiling, and Danni looked at him doubtfully. Hard to say whether that was an accusation or a compliment.

She said crossly, 'I'm not posing for your entertainment if that's what you mean.'

'No? You mean you aren't even trying?'

She didn't like the way he stood there, face carefully unexpressive, watching her silently. It reminded her uncannily of last night, and that was something she didn't want to be reminded of. She took a quick step towards her pile of dishes, a dodging movement that was unfortunately spoiled by a projecting root that tripped her. Instead of putting distance between them she fell headlong into Jay's arms, and he wasn't slow to fasten them around her.

He held her body pressed so close to his that her ears picked up the rise and fall of his breathing, the throbbing of his heart. Danni gasped, and he slackened his grip, holding her with one hand, trailing the fingers of the other slowly, sensuously, along her jawline and letting it travel lightly over her neck and throat, and down— all the time half smiling—and Danni made her defensive move impulsively, wrenching herself back quickly out of his easier grasp.

A tree-trunk barred her way and she backed against it, crossing her breasts with her hands as she faced him, as if she might have expected assault.

'Don't be silly.' His voice was husky. 'You look like an outraged virgin,' and because she felt foolish Danni let him slide his hands around her body and press her again towards him.

His hand came between them, brushing her breasts, and she felt the power of him even through the cotton dress she wore, touching her lightly, but setting her on fire.

'Not every woman has real magic,' he murmured, bending his head so that his lips were close to her ear. 'What a pity it had to be you, Danni Paige. You're a real heart-stopper. I can hardly believe anybody could be so dramatic and sexually disturbing without even trying. Are you trying, Danni?'

This was the kind of talk Danni could well do without. It was time to pull away, the signals were all there. Yet something kept her standing there, in the circle of his arm, staring at him, with the red sky and the dark trees making a scene of almost incredible drama around them, and the dark man looking down at her out of those narrowed eyes that could be screening any kind of feeling or intention at all.

She knew he wanted to hold and touch her, that he was feeling a wanting, and that she had probably triggered it off because he happened to look up and see her standing there, silhouetted against the scarlet end of a long and emotional day.

He didn't like her, she was sure of that. And he didn't trust her. So why was he here?

It was almost as if he heard her silent question; when he spoke he could have been answering.

'Something is happening between us, Danni. You feel it, too. You must. You felt it last night.'

Why couldn't she move? The danger signs were all there, Jay recovering from his bout of anger, emotionally stirred by his meeting with the Aboriginal elder, perhaps not reasoning so clearly as usual.

He bent again and kissed her hair, and this was definitely her cue to make a move for safety, yet something held her there, immobilised. The breath that stirred her hair was ragged and uneven, warm as the day had been, and as he pressed her against his body once again Danni heard the pounding of his heart. Why couldn't she act?

Docile, she let Jay cradle her head with his fingers on the nape of her neck and slowly, languorously, as if he relished every moment, brush his lips against her defenceless mouth, lightly at first, then with a sudden fierceness that broke down the last of Danni's defences.

This was sensation as she had never known it, and she felt herself surrendering, her heart pounding with excitement and expectation.

Jay wanted her... oh yes, he did. She could feel the wanting. This was no exercise in seduction, no deliberate stirring of her senses so that he could reject her and teach her a lesson. Jay wanted her as much at this moment as she wanted him. She saw the desire flaming in his eyes. The wanting showed plainly in his body language, the hunger in his feverish touching.

Spellbound, motivated by forces far beyond her control, Danni freed her arms and raised them, twining them slowly and sensuously around Jay's strong neck, absorbing the strength of him with a surge of pleasure that sent the last remnant of self-control dissolving in a wave of pleasure.

As her fingers tangled in the thick black curls on the nape of his neck, Jay convulsively pulled her even closer to him, and before she knew what was happening he had unbuttoned his shirt and Danni found her cheek crushed against the crisp curls on his chest. She turned her head so that her mouth made contact with the tanned skin, feeling a ripple of pleasure run through his body.

They were setting each other alight. Everywhere he touched her body sang with instant awareness. Her breasts throbbed and deep in her body an upsurge of longing, part physical, part emotional, burst into vibrant life, like a showerburst of stars.

His body moved against hers, and anything might have happened then, because Danni had become unaware of anything except her passion flaring, her need of Jay. They were a fraction away from complete loss of control, when Jay drew one deep, shuddering breath and moved his hands from her body. It was like losing a limb—some part of herself.

Slowly Jay eased away from her, and Danni stiffened, unbelieving. Was he going to do it again—play out the great rejection scene? She stifled the protest that crowded her throat.

Jay reached out one hand and laid it on her head, palm down. He let one small muffled sound escape him before he spoke.

'Time to cool it,' he ordered. 'If I were to seduce you, Danni Paige, your mother would be after me with all guns blazing.'

Anger rose in Danni like a wild tide. 'And that would scare you?' she scoffed. 'Like hell it would!'

She stared at him, disbelieving what she saw. How could he call a halt to the experience they had seemed so wonderfully close to sharing? How could he put out the fires so quickly? He looked cool enough now, standing there with the red sky fading all around him, with that cryptic, almost humorous twist to his lips.

'Time to retire. Into our separate tents, I mean. And don't go standing against any more sunsets, Danielle, or I can't vouch for my continued good behaviour. A man can take just so much.' As if it had been her fault, as if she had been the temptress... Danni bent to gather up the washed dishes, holding them in the crook of one arm, and surprisingly Jay curled his fingers around the other wrist as they walked slowly back to the camp site where the small tents stood beside two spreading gum trees in the gathering shadows.

Jay let her wrist go. 'Don't be disturbed if you hear scufflings in the night. Lionel will let us know if we should take action about anything. He's the expert on intruders of all sizes, but there's nothing dangerous around here.'

Only you, Danni thought as she stacked away the dishes. And heaven knows you're dangerous enough.

After everything was tidied up she collected her sleeping-bag and mumbled about an early night and feeling tired, and Jay could make what he liked of it, because she was having her own way this time, and taking refuge in her tent. Maybe that was cowardly but that was her decision.

Only of course she didn't sleep at once. She lay awake wondering about a lot of things: about Jay's alarming potency and her own reaction to it, about tomorrow and whether it would bring any hassles.

She had always promised herself that when she chose a man it would be for love and commitment, like her father and mother; but she had certainly under-estimated the power of passion and physical attraction. Was that something she ought to experience more fully before she decided on the direction her life must take?

Danni liked pleasant sensation, but Jay North obviously lived in a world of sensuality and experience far more potent than she was used to. Maybe she wasn't ready for that kind of experience yet? The collecting of emotional scars was something she had managed to dodge so far, and every instinct warned that you didn't tangle with Jackson North and his kind without some changes being made to your life and outlook.

An affair with Jay North could be an enriching experience, something to remember on cold winter nights. Or it could leave a haunting, painful sense of loss that would stay forever tender, ready to stir in a renewal of pain whenever life presented her with some reminder.

Danni knew about that. She had watched this aspect growing in her mother over the years since her father's passing, seeing her retreat into a world of sadness whenever she remembered him. So perhaps she wasn't ready to enter Jay's world yet. Perhaps she needed a little more time.

When the shadow fell across her tent Danni knew Jay was out there. Her heart leaped as he lifted the flap of her tent, his face a pale blur in the shadows, but he only said,

'Thought I'd better tell you, if I'm not in sight when you wake in the morning don't be alarmed. I'm going after our tail. We've been shadowed long enough. I'll wager that little green sneaky varmint isn't far away.' He gave a faint smile in the darkness. 'You appear to have softened my urge to destroy for the moment. If it's your brother, I'll let him off with a caution before I send him packing.'

'And if it's Derek?' Danni couldn't resist the challenge, but Jay's glance was shrewd. Even in the darkness she could feel his mockery.

'If it's your devoted lover I'll probably flatten his head to pulp before I give him the boot. You won't object too strongly, I hope.'

But he didn't imagine for one moment it was Derek, and he didn't hide the cynical note in his voice, and Danni fumed.

'I'm sure you'll do whatever takes your fancy. You don't care whether it will bother me or not,' she retorted tersely. He didn't bother to deny it, merely gave a derisive grin and a mocking 'Sweet dreams, sweet lady,' before he disappeared. She heard him whistle for Lionel and move away.

Did she wish he would come back? That was something that didn't bear thinking about, and she tossed it quickly out of her mind. No, he was trouble, and the farther away he stayed, the safer she would be.

Neither Jay nor Lionel was in sight when Danni woke up next morning. She washed and dressed, then took down her tent and folded her sleeping-bag.

She was cooking breakfast when Jay came through the trees, Lionel scampering at his heels, and he looked more than slightly pleased with himself.

Danni's heart sank. Not Gregg, she prayed silently...

She had no idea how vulnerable she looked standing in arrested motion, wide-eyed, waiting to hear what he had to say.

Jay settled himself on a camp-stool, helped himself to a mug of tea from the boiling billy before he drawled with almost over-stated casualness,

'Seems I owe you an apology, Danielle.'

'It isn't Gregg!' Not until last night had Danni really allowed herself to admit that it could have been her young brother, urged on by some mistaken belief that she needed him to protect her, who was making such a clumsy effort to keep them under surveillance.

Out here with only scattered undergrowth to offer concealment nobody could hope to remain undetected for long, not even an expert, and the person following them was certainly no expert.

Jay took in the slow relaxation of Danni's soft mouth, the undisguised relief flooding her eyes, before he went on, still playing it casual,

'I appear to have made a blunder.'

'Not the great Jackson North!'

'Don't be cheeky.' He flicked her cheek with an indolent finger as he passed to refill his tea-mug, and Danni's heart jerked. It must be her imagination, she told herself fiercely, but there seemed an intimacy about that lazy gesture, something in the way he smiled at her, the gleam that flashed in those usually cool grey eyes, that suggested something between them had changed for the better.

He carried his tea back to the stool. 'Seems that young assistant I hired and lost didn't go back to his folks after all. He's on our tail, with friend.'

Danni stared at him, bewildered.

'Why ever would he do that? Why would anybody want to follow us?'

'I can think of only one likely reason. I checked over my itinerary with him, roughly of course, but I did disclose that I had to visit the man I told your family about, the old battler who owns the pub and store out in the middle of nowhere. He's been trying to sell his property, such as it is, for so long he's brought the price down to rock bottom, and still no takers. Like an idiot I told my prospective new assistant about the good news I have for him. I got some inside information that the Government plans to extend two highways, and they'll meet right at his pub when they're finished.' Jay grinned. 'I wouldn't mind buying it myself. His pub will be at the junction. Can you imagine how trade will leap out of sight? All the coaches full of tourists stopping for food and drinks and souvenirs. He'll have a thriving business on his hands.'

Jay put down the empty mug of tea, helped himself to eggs and bacon, tossed Lionel a few scraps.

'I tried to reach Wattie by radio phone but it seems he's out prospecting and the handyman he left in charge couldn't reach him. But if these guys behind us get to him first no doubt they figure to make a killing, buy the business at a low price and reap the profits. He's a great old battler, Wattie. I don't propose to stand by and see him fleeced.'

'Why don't they go straight there, whoever they are?'

Jay's mouth twisted. 'That's the one thing I did right. They don't know the exact location, so they have to hang on our tail until we lead them close, which I don't propose to do. Wattie's had a hard life and he deserves a break after spending years in a dead town—talk about the ends of the earth——'

He finished his meal, and finished what packing Danni hadn't done.

'We'll have to rearrange our schedule and get our business with Wattie done as soon as we can.' He watched Danni impatiently as she searched for sunglasses. 'How do you feel about standing up to a rough ride?'

'How rough? Do I need cushions?'

'I'll arrange the sleeping-bags behind you to act as extra shock absorbers.'

Danni saw then why Jackson North had to become an explorer, an achiever who surmounted obstacles and overcame challenges. His whole body was vibrant with energy, his movements tensed and quickened.

He whistled softly as he arranged the sleeping-bag behind Danni and cushioned Lionel between them, and the exhilaration was catching. Danni smiled back at him cheerfully.

'Something to tell my grandchildren,' she offered brightly. 'And if I collect any bruises I'll sue you.'

'Better than that, I'll attend to them for you myself.'

That was either a promise or a threat, depending how you looked at it. Danni sat with assumed ease beside Jay as he set the four-wheel-drive in motion. For a while they travelled along a fairly smooth if dusty roadway between what looked like interminable miles of flat land, then suddenly Jay swung off the road across a cattle grid and waited for Danni to alight and open the gate. There were no cattle in sight, only a rough and winding track that seemed to lead across the high spiky grass to a range of mountains.

Dust rose in a cloud behind them. Their trailing driver would have no difficulty locating the direction in which they travelled.

When they reached the long, long line of stark and rocky peaks Jay grunted happily. 'There's a tricky bit of track here. It goes between two of the sheerest peaks and I think that's where we'll lose our trailers. There's no other way through. Our transport is heavier and more powerful than theirs so I'm hoping they won't make it.'

He gave a quick look over his shoulder and grunted again.

'They're here, I can see the dust. Now hang on to your seat and try not to look back. They don't know

I'm on to them. I crept up on their camp in the dark.
They were sleeping out in the open—very handy for the
observer.'

He gave a taciturn grin. 'I rather fancy myself after
that neat bit of detection. Lucky for me they didn't have
a dog to sound the alarm.'

The big four-wheel-drive lumbered precariously over
what looked like anything but a track. They tilted slowly
over potholes, some of them filled with red dust. They
crawled at terrifying angles over bumpy rocks and Danni
closed her eyes then opened them again. If they were
going to stand on their heads she might as well see it
happen.

Danni knew about bull-dust, the deceptive fine sand
that filled holes, turning them into traps for the unwary
driver who expected a solid surface but found himself
instead floundering in a steep-sided crater. So that was
the man-trap that Jay hoped to lead his unwelcome 'tail'
into, no doubt.

Danni hung on to her seat-belt as they climbed noisily
out of one very large hole, and Jay looked back at the
cloud of settling dust and grunted with satisfaction.

'They shouldn't get out of this one. It'll take them a
while, anyway. Long enough for us to lose them.'

He drove to the end of the pass, left Danni and Lionel
in the Range Rover, and doubled back on foot, walking
lightly, to see how the smaller vehicle had fared. When
he came back he had a broad grin that signified some
kind of triumph.

'We've lost them. They'll be there for ages. Now all
we have to do is get back to the road and get on with
what we should be doing.'

When they were once more pointed in the right
direction Jay pulled up on their side of the road. A short
radio conversation ensured that a couple of stockmen

from the property would later ride out to give assistance
to the stranded men and their vehicle if they needed it.

Satisfied, and obviously pleased with his morning's
work, Jay opened the car fridge and poured cold drinks
for them both. 'In case you're feeling frazzled.'

His expression was quizzical and Danni took a couple
of sips of the liquid gratefully before she announced,
'You don't give a damn whether I'm frazzled or not.'

She was horrified to feel a faint tremor shaking the
fingers that held the cold glass, and she steadied them
fiercely, because nothing—but nothing—was going to
let the man know that she might be shaken.

But she shivered inwardly, studying his harsh face in
the morning sunlight, seeing again the out-thrust jaw,
the narrowed eyes, feeling the determination—no, what
was the word?—implacability—as he led his victim into
the trap. She would hate to become Jackson North's
enemy. He would be a merciless foe, and so powerful.

It threw her when he slanted her a look over the rim
of his glass and asked casually, 'Bet you're not brave
enough to tell me what you decided then in your pretty
little thoughts.'

Danni put down her glass, and he opened another
bottle of cool drink and handed Danni the refilled glass.

'So?' he queried silkily.

'They weren't pretty little thoughts. I was just deciding you would make one hell of an enemy. You really
enjoy flattening somebody into the dust, don't you?'

'Only when they offend me. I can be really nice, if
you treat me right.'

He studied her lazily, deliberately letting his gaze linger
on Danni's slender fingers wrapped around her glass,
watching her expression teasingly as she locked and
unlocked her fingers, uneasy because of the lingering
intentness of his gaze.

Finally he said softly, 'You think of me at present in terms of enmity, but you know what they say—yesterday's enemy, tomorrow's lover.'

'Nonsense. I don't believe anybody ever said that. If they did they didn't know what they were talking about.'

Danni finished her drink quickly, and when Jay offered casually, 'Another refill?' she shook her head, deciding thankfully that he now considered the subject of enemies that turned into lovers was closed for the time being.

Tomorrow's lover... she hoped uneasily that wasn't what he had in mind.

Gregg had been right, she should have listened to his warning and not ventured on this treacherous journey with this dangerous man, not at any price.

CHAPTER SEVEN

THEY reached Wattie's property late that afternoon and Danni's immediate reaction was, 'No wonder the man wants to sell. Who would live here?'

The old wooden buildings cried out for a coat of paint, the windows were blurred and dusty, and although everything else was clean and cared for, there was an air of desolation about the place. There was actually an ancient utility refuelling at the one and only pump as they arrived. An old man in overalls finished the job and nodded his head in answer to the laconic, 'Book it, will you, Herb?' from the driver, before he turned to talk to Jay.

He raised both eyebrows comically when he saw Danni alighting from the vehicle, then turned his attention to Jay.

'Wattie ain't here,' he announced tersely. 'Should be back later today though. I saw his fire last night, up on old Fortitude—that's the hill way out there——' He waved a wrinkled hand towards a range of distant mountains. 'Probably take him all day to get back here but he ought to make it before sunset.'

Grumbling under his breath, he offered refreshment, and Danni soon realised the muttering was a habit, a long-ingrained fashion of talking to himself. He muttered continually while he poured their drinks and produced a snack.

But Jay was restless. When the old man grumbled his way into the kitchen he pushed his chair back abruptly.

'Will you be all right here? I'll have a talk to Herb then go out and meet Wattie. I've made a few notes you might type out for me.' He grinned wickedly. 'Did them after you went to bed last night. Meanwhile you might tell the old codger to rub that "For Sale" sign off the window, and not—repeat not—accept any offers. Not that he can act without Wattie anyway.'

He smiled at her lazily. 'I'll be back before nightfall. Wattie can't be all that far away. You heard what Herb said.'

He fetched the typewriter and set it up on a small table in the ancient bar-room, watched by an interested Herb.

'You don't object to watching over my assistant while I'm away?' Jay queried, and Herb gave a wink.

'No trouble at all. I'll see nobody carries her off.'

He directed his next cheerful wink towards Danni. 'Go for your life, girl. We aren't likely to be interrupted. We've had our one and only caller for the day.'

Danni knew she should have been relieved when Jay set off on the motorcycle, heading towards the distant hills, but perversely she felt deprived by his departure, almost lonely although Herb was bustling about, and she set to work typing vigorously, determined not to think about him riding so fast away from her, and eventually she lost track of time and even blotted out the sound of Herbie's monotonous grumbling as he wandered around the empty bar, swatting at occasional flies and dusting tables that would soon dust over again as the late afternoon breeze stirred up the thirsty landscape.

It was almost evening when Danni heard the sound of the returning motorcycle. Her jobs were done, and she had managed a quick shower under hard yellowish water that made her skin feel tight and her hair stringy.

She used skin balm and perfumed talc generously, and swept her hair back with a coloured scarf tied in a graceful bow on the back of her neck, and when she changed into a white cotton skirt and flowered body shirt she might not have felt elegant but at least she was clean and refreshed.

When Jay walked in he grinned. 'Hello! Very sexy!' He meant she didn't look at all sexy and she pulled a face at him, but the lean, sun-tanned bushman who walked in behind him did not realise the comment was loaded.

He said, 'I think so too, miss,' and when Jay introduced them he held her hand in his weathered fingers and Danni saw only genuine admiration in his eyes.

He could have been any age between fifty and seventy, his thin brown hair was grey-streaked, the skin around his eyes wrinkled in brown and white lines, but he held himself upright and his eyes were keen. He had probably looked like this for years, it was difficult to judge the lean and sinewy weather-tanned men of the outback, Danni knew that already.

Herbie grunted welcome to Wattie. 'Find anything?'

'Couple of sightings. Nothing to set the world on fire. Wasn't worth the effort, I guess,' Wattie answered his mate. 'But I had to get away for a bit. My feet get the wanders every now and then.'

He grinned cheerfully at Danni. 'The news your boss brought me was a darn sight better than anything I could find out there. What are we eating, Herb?'

Herbie said, 'Stew' and Wattie grimaced at Jay, as if he might have heard that answer many times before. He murmured, 'Surprise!' before he stowed his gear and went for a wash-up.

When he came back he poured drinks, including a long cold one for himself, and Herbie jerked a thumb towards the windows.

'Cleaned your sale sign off,' he explained laconically.

'I noticed that.' Wattie's eyes twinkled. 'Added ten years to me life, that did. Must say I feel sprightlier than

I've felt for a long time. Can't thank you two enough for coming out of your way to give us the good news.'

He included Danni in his gratitude but it was towards Jay that the real warmth of his thanks was directed. He didn't use many words but his feeling showed in the respectful slap on the shoulder, the glint in those keen bright eyes as he listened to Jay talking, the eager way he served both of them with the evening meal, taking care they enjoyed it, watchful they had everything they needed.

He offered them room to sleep, part of a screened-off portion of the veranda, a little embarrassed because it was the only space ready for occupation, relieved when Jay explained he and Danni were used to sleeping wherever they found themselves.

As they sat having a nightcap Wattie said thoughtfully, 'I'd better get busy on the garden tomorrow, seeing as I'm gonna be around here a long time yet, if I'm lucky.' He downed his drink with relish, admitting ruefully, 'I've rather let things go.'

'Won't you be lonely?' Danni asked without thinking. He hesitated.

'Well—actually—that was the reason I was trying to sell. Not that I was lonely myself—never that—but my wife, she up and left the place some years ago when our three sons grew up and left us. She got kinda fed up with it being so quiet here, and nobody much ever around. I could see her point, so it seemed after a while that the decent thing for me to do was to sell up and go look for her.' A wry grin flickered over his rough features. 'Mind you, I took my time about it, didn't I? Seven years . . . but we kept in touch, I get a letter now and then, and I figured one day we'd work something out.'

There was a moist brightness in his eyes, a lightness in his voice, as he reached out and touched Jay's arm.

'Now, thanks to you, sport, I might be able to persuade her to come back, if things are going to get livelier. Bit of company besides mine now and then, that was all she wanted. Yes, that was it.' He seemed quite sure of that. 'That was all she missed really, seeing people come and go. But I mustn't bore you folks. You'll be wanting your rest.'

'You're right about that.' Jay pushed back his chair and stood up. 'We'll make an early start in the morning. Don't worry if you're not about. We won't need anything.'

Wattie looked as if that might be a bit of a joke, anybody getting up earlier than he did.

'I'll be there.'

His eyes twinkled at Danni as he moved away, and Danni walked with Jay to a small space on the veranda where two single beds lay side by side.

Jay grinned wickedly. 'You are safe, fair maiden.' He crossed his heart as Danni hesitated beside the first bed. She didn't feel safe.

She watched him warily as he fumbled in his overnight bag. He lifted his head and looked at her across the width of the two beds and a faint smile played about his lips as he tossed toilet gear on to the bed.

'I'll tell you this, Danielle. If you were mine and you left me, it wouldn't take me seven years to get off my tail and drag you back to where you belonged. They don't hurry things, do they, these old-timers?'

He was smiling as he turned away, leaving her with the thought. Then he began to whistle softly as he prepared for bed, taking off his shirt, unbuttoning his shorts. Danni watched him covertly because she couldn't help it, her senses absorbing the sight of his tanned back, taut-muscled, narrow-waisted, the broad shoulders and sleek hips giving out an aura of strength and power that came across even in the lazy movements of undressing.

As Jay began dropping his shorts Danni averted her gaze quickly. She felt rather than saw him walk past her to the washroom.

She sat on the edge of her bed, brushing her hair. What was she supposed to do—climb into bed and wait for his return? Oh no, she wasn't that foolish. She brushed long and hard until he returned, ignoring the ironic lift of his dark brows as he passed her.

As he peeled off his briefs Danni averted her gaze quickly. If Jay noticed her furtive glances he gave no sign, but settled himself in the other bed and lay with his back to her.

Only then, when she saw Jay apparently settled and ready for sleep, did Danni change into her short cotton nightshirt. She lay in bed watching the moon-silvered sky through the tiny geometric patterns of the wire screening that covered the windows. She kept very quiet. Being thrown by circumstances into this small sleeping-space with Jay so close beside her made her feel unsettled. She didn't know what to expect.

Now the relaxed body on the bed beside hers told her what to expect—just nothing. The man obviously intended getting to sleep as quickly as he could.

Stealthily, Danni plumped up her pillow so that she could raise her head and look out at the contrast of the shadowed veranda and the silvery world outside.

It came to her then, as she drifted in the tranquil world of half-sleep half-awakening, that this wonderful feeling of serenity could have something to do with the blurred figure in the bed beside hers, and she pushed the suggestion away hastily. This was no time to soften.

Once Jay stirred, only a little, just enough to make Danni hold her breath until he settled down again. Just as she thought him deep in sleep again, and no more danger to her peace of mind, he spoke.

'Goodnight, Danielle,' he murmured softly, with the faintest tinge of amusement in his voice.

Danni feigned sleep, breathing slowly and regularly. Of course she wasn't fooling him, but at least she wasn't giving him any encouragement; and after a while there was no sound on the dark veranda but the soft rise and fall of two people breathing peacefully, fast asleep.

They left behind an exuberant and grateful Wattie in the early hours of next morning. Herbie had sandwiches ready and he even offered a covered basin of left-over stew which Jay refused tactfully, saying they were cramped for space.

Wattie winked cheerfully. He knew Herbie's stews were not exactly gourmet fare, but nothing could dampen his spirits this morning. Already he was making plans to leave Herbie in charge while he went off to find his estranged wife, to tell her the good news and try to lure her back.

'She'll probably come, after a bit of coaxing,' Jay commented as he swung on to an uneven dirt road, sending a flock of scarlet and green parrots fluttering in an agitated whirlwind of colour.

'How do you know?' Danni asked curiously.

'The people of the outback develop a special need of the vast open country. I can see why Wattie's wife couldn't stay while he wasn't making a decent living. It must have seemed futile to her, and she wanted to be near her children, maybe grandchildren in due time; but with prospects of a good future and something to work for I'll be surprised if she doesn't come back to him.'

'Typical male attitude,' Danni challenged. 'Suppose she has met somebody else? She could have, you know.'

Jay took his time about answering. 'That's a possibility, of course, but outback people are very loyal. They don't talk much about their feelings, some of them don't talk much about anything, but love and loyalties run deep and true. I shouldn't be surprised if Wattie's wife has been jogging along just the same as Wattie, hoping for a miracle to bring them together again.

Danni thought about this as the country changed, and they began to cross a stony plain.

'Where are we headed?'

'We're heading farther west and south, to what is almost desert country, so you'd better keep your sun-hat handy.'

Jay kept his wide-brimmed stockman's hat handy most of the time, although he hadn't used it much up to date. He said, 'We aren't in a hurry now we've seen Wattie. I've a couple of isolated spots to call at. A friend of mine is interested in wildlife, she paints for a hobby, and I promised to photograph some of the wildlife, especially birds, around the waterholes. I might have been able to show you some brolgas dancing but I'm not sure whether it's the right time of the year.' He smiled at her obliquely. 'I understand they show off best in the mating season, like most of us.'

Danni found herself wishing she had brought her own camera. Derek would have been delighted with wildlife pictures, but she had been so anxious to travel light that her luggage consisted only of essentials.

However, she did use some of her notebooks to make quick sketches that could be a source of possible ideas for souvenirs.

For the next couple of days, as they drove over rugged countryside, exploring occasional waterholes or caves or rock formations, Danni found herself becoming more and more involved with her work. The heat did not bother her nearly as much as she had feared, and between making script revisions and additions, helping set up cameras, taking notes and cooking meals, she found time passing swiftly, filled with interest.

Behind the superficial monotony of some parts of the landscape there were, she discovered, a great many surprises, and she found herself enjoying the strange new world Jackson North had led her into. That was a mistake. She should have known better.

On the third day they set up camp beside a long stretch of scrubby country, and when Jay announced plans to leave Danni typing while he drove away to take more film, he said slyly, 'You needn't feel nervous left on your own. I'm leaving Lionel to guard you. If you finish the job and fancy a bit of exploration you can take him for a walk, but don't get yourself lost, and don't go far.'

Of course she wouldn't go far, she wasn't all that foolish, and she would take good care not to get lost because that would give Jackson North a chance to show his superiority, and that just wasn't to be thought of.

But when her work was finished Danni folded the table and leaned it against a tree, stowing the typewriter away in her tent.

The little dog had waited patiently. Now he gave a short bark, frisked a few paces toward the scrubby trees, and looked back at her.

'All right. Wait until I get my hat.'

Danni hadn't yet established a true friendship with Lionel. They were acquaintances but with polite reservations. Maybe he took his cue from his master, and this might be a good chance to improve their relationship. She let Lionel lead her among the grass and trees.

Danni was careful not to lose direction. To have Jackson North forced to conduct a personal search for her was the last thing she desired. He had warned her to watch for cattle because there was a shallow waterhole not far away, but none were visible. A blue kingfisher watched from a branch in a dead treetop, and

Danni marked his tree in her mind as a pointer to their camp site when she and Lionel returned.

She walked cautiously through the long dry grass, watchful for snakes, although Jay had not mentioned them as a possible hazard, but the last thing she wanted was to be a liability. She must not get lost, she must not get snake-bitten, and she could imagine no other risks so she and Lionel walked up one small hill and down the other side, and when Danni saw the grey four-wheel-drive parked in a clump of trees near a patch of sand in the middle of the valley, she felt enormously pleased with herself. By pure coincidence it looked as if she had done the right thing this time. For some ridiculous reason she was actually pleased to find Jay.

She whistled to Lionel and they headed for the sand on the valley floor. They didn't hurry. The sun was hot, and Danni pushed the green sun-hat back from her forehead and gathered up her loose hair into a coil on the back of her neck, brushing small beads of perspiration from her cheeks.

She noted wryly that her feet began to move more quickly as they came closer to the Range Rover, and deliberately made herself slow down as they reached the sand. But not Lionel! He leaped across the sand, barking excitedly, and suddenly a swift small grey shape reared up in front of him. A frill-necked lizard, body erect, his frill fully extended in grotesque fantasy, barred their path.

Danni did a quick turnabout, backing into the grasses, unable to prevent herself stumbling into an object behind her. It was only when she turned and saw the fallen tripod with the camera beside it that she realised how horribly she had blundered.

The reptile continued to dance his aggression at the intruders. Lionel's bright eyes watched Danni, awaiting orders. She said 'Sit,' trying to put into her voice some of Jackson's authority, and it must have worked, because Lionel sat obediently.

Camera and tripod lay in the dust. The frill-necked lizard, having made his spectacular gesture of defiance, made himself scarce among the grasses. Jay came suddenly on to the scene from behind the trees, just in time to see the scene of disaster. He swore.

'Damnation! Do you know how long it took me to set that up, you—you stupid——'

Danni met his fury chin up although her stomach was lurching.

'Bitch,' she finished off for him, when he left the sentence hanging. Some of the fire went out of him. Not much, but it told Danni she had scored a point. He muttered, 'If you say so,' and then, 'Heaven knows when we'll get a chance of another shot like that.'

He gave an exaggerated sigh, and Danni received another glare.

'Everybody's little helper,' he muttered. 'You surely are walking disasters, you Paiges. What the hell did you think you were doing?'

'It was an accident.' Danni moistened dry lips.

'I certainly hope so.' He didn't look convinced.

Danni ventured, 'If you hadn't left your camera unattended...' but it was a pathetic effort, and Jay demolished it swiftly.

'You mean, all this is entirely my own fault?' Grey eyes glittered under the broad brim of the stockman's hat. He was angry enough to explode. Even through her dismay Danni registered the beads of perspiration on his hands and face. He was hot and he was cross. No doubt he had stalked his lizard, crawling through sand and grass, quite some time, and Danni realised with deadly shame that it would be quite a long time before he found a replacement.

He pushed the hat high on his forehead, and glowered at her. Danni told herself she wasn't remorseful but there was a hollow feeling in her stomach. She did feel guilty and ashamed, and for the first time actually considered asking Jackson North to let her off the rest of the work. He could take the caravan park—it wasn't worth it.

Her dismay deepened as she felt the tell-tale quivering of her lips, and she sniffed, and opened her mouth to tell him what he could do with his job, only the words stuck in her throat.

He snarled at her. 'Get yourself together, for heaven's sake. You might try picking up the mess you've made.'

He looked pointedly at the camera and because she was in no mood for defiance Danni grabbed it and began blowing red dust off the cover, scanning the lens with concern.

'I can't see any sand on it. Could it be damaged?'

'We don't know, do we?'

A little of the anger had gone out of him but he was still punishing her. Lionel sat immobile behind Danni's left leg, trying to look inconspicuous. He knew something had gone dreadfully wrong. Instinct told him this was no longer a play-day.

When Danni moved and handed the camera to Jay for his inspection the dog leaned his head on his front paws and gazed first at Danni, then at Jay, with bright enquiring eyes.

Danni asked in a small voice, 'Mightn't it—the lizard—mightn't it come back?' and Jay snarled, 'Not very likely, is it, with Lionel's scent all over the place. That's why I left him with you in the first place.'

The deceit of the man! I'll leave Lionel to guard you, he had said. Two-faced! Danni studied the tanned granite face furiously. Who did he think he was?

Jay jerked his head towards the parked vehicle.

'Get in. I'll drive you back.'

'I'll walk back, thank you.'

'And fall over a snake?' His face was grim. 'Or down a mine shaft?'

'A mine shaft! I didn't know there were any,' Danni offered, interested, then seeing the thunder on his face she choked quickly before turning her back on him.

'I'll meet you back at the camp.' She fired her last defiant shot before walking determinedly over the tufted grass towards the trees. Lionel wavered uncomfortably before deciding that loyalty to his master came first, and with an apologetic twitch of his tail followed on Jay's heels.

Of course the man reached camp well before her. He seemed to take malicious pleasure watching her step warily between the scratchy branches of twisted trees, her face flushed and damp with perspiration, tendrils of hair curling moistly against her cheeks.

But Danni was ready for him, all guns blazing. How dare he suggest she was clumsy because of one stupid and unfortunate mistake? And worse still, there had been a suggestion of deliberate sabotage in that scathing, 'I hope so,' when she had explained it was an accident.

Yet to Danni's surprise as she approached he foraged in the back of the Range Rover and came back with a spare stockman's hat, broad-brimmed and shady, which he offered to her with a faint quirk of his lips.

'Better take this. That green object on your head isn't doing much in the way of protection. This is no time to get sunstroke.'

The 'green object' on her head was made of straw, and definitely not so good at offering a shield for her face as the large hat he offered her, so Danni did not argue.

Jay didn't say another word about the overturned camera or the ruined shots, and Danni scrutinised him suspiciously. When she made no move to take the hat from him he reached out and removed the green hat from her head and replaced it with the stockman's gear, arranging it carefully on her head, strong brown fingers dipping the wide brim to make a veranda over her forehead.

'That's better.' He stepped back to inspect the effect. 'Very fetching. And it should keep you on the job.'

She knew she looked hot and bothered and discouraged, and she eyed him doubtfully before offering a reluctant, 'Thanks.'

She didn't like Jay behaving in this unexpected manner, deciding with surprise that she preferred hostility, because she could always counter his anger with her own, and thus keep them apart.

But this offhand friendly gesture threw her off balance, especially after the blast he had handed her a few minutes ago. She didn't know what to think or what to expect.

She said awkwardly, 'I'm sorry about the pictures I spoiled. I suppose it was careless,' and he raised ironic eyebrows.

'No suppose about it. It was careless. But you won't do it again, I'm sure.'

No, she wouldn't do it again, Danni decided waspishly. She would watch her steps carefully in future. He was being extraordinarily magnanimous about her carelessness.

She supposed that was rather big of him and almost repeated her apology, then was glad she hadn't, because he suddenly moved so close she could see the smudges of sweat and dust on his cheeks, and his right hand shot out and grasped her chin, tilting her face so that the screening hat no longer threw its shadow over her eyes.

'What is it about you, Danielle, that gets to me, I wonder? What do you have that no other woman has?'

'Nothing.' Danni pushed him away flatly. 'I don't want to—to get to you—as you call it—believe me——'

He laughed, a short hard laugh, watching her still with that intent gaze, searching her features as if he sought something behind her expression.

'That's the problem, Danni. I don't know whether to believe you or not. After all, you're Ryan Paige's daughter
'

He moved even closer to her. 'Don't you fancy me at all, Danni? Don't you feel what's happening between us?'

'No, I don't. I don't want to——'

'I could make you ...'

He was threatening her. Even as she straightened her shoulders, prepared to launch another verbal assault, to tell him she wouldn't like his kind of man in a million years, he made his swift move and pinioned her so close against him she felt the sweat-dampness of his shirt, the muscle-movement as he tightened his arms.

He kissed her fiercely, taking her lips with his own hot mouth, holding her immobile while he moved his body gently against hers.

Deep in her own body Danni felt the involuntary response, the deep springing of desire she had no power to control.

Jay moved his mouth eventually away from hers, slowly, the heat of both their bodies making the soft lips cling together as if they separated with reluctance. A triumphant gleam flashed in his eyes.

'See?' he goaded.

With a superhuman effort Danni used her anger to lash out with her arms, turning her body sideways to use its strength to push him away.

Taken by surprise by the sudden strong movement, Jay found himself pushed away a short distance. He didn't lose balance, just stood there looking at her, legs slightly apart, a gleam of something in his eyes that could have been admiration but just might have been mockery.

Danni jammed the cowboy hat down over her face. Her green eyes flashed. 'I might have known! I really fell for it, didn't I? The great Jackson North sporting a chivalrous streak, worrying about whether I got sunstroke. Hah!'

Hands on hips, chin jutting furiously, the cowboy hat jammed hard on her head, Danni forgot her embarrassment and faced her tormentor. His grin mocked her.

'Anger becomes you. There is a vibrancy I have never seen in anybody else. You come alive when you're angry.' He gestured to Lionel to follow him. 'Now, how about something to eat?'

So that was it. End of scene. He moved nonchalantly away and began putting up the stove and the gas cylinder, indicating to Danni that she was responsible for the meal. He poured two cold glasses of beer, a wry twist of his lips suggesting that she needed one, and Danni accepted hers crossly, but she was glad of the cold, refreshing liquid that somehow took the edge off her anger and resentment and allowed her to carry on as if those two rattling scenes they had just played had never taken place.

She would forget the ruined footage and the spilled camera, and she would also put the impertinence of Jay's overtures, and his arrogance, into some special place in her mind where it would not be forgotten—oh no, that was a memory she must keep as a warning—but she would not do him the favour of letting herself be thrown off balance by his damned cheek, his overgrown assurance.

Jay became surprisingly casual over the next few days. His manner became so bland that Danni told herself uneasily several times it must be too good to last. Could he be playing a waiting game? Then the sunlight would drive her doubts away and she settled down to the routine of note-keeping, watching and learning.

The nights were different. Danni watched the fall of darkness uneasily, only too aware that if he wanted to Jackson North could bring into those dark and starry hours a quality of excitement that set her heart leaping every time he announced with apparent casualness, 'Bedtime, I think, don't you?'

Yet he made no move. Danni was almost lulled into that security she had warned herself against when they found themselves at a pleasant bubbling pool among an oasis of greenery. Danni was enchanted.

Tree-trunks had fallen across the pool, and running water bubbled under them and over them in swirling cascades. Jay watched Danni kneeling at the water's edge, dipping her fingers into the eddies.

'It's thermal,' he explained, 'a spring of warm water. You can stay and have a swim if you like. I don't need you where I'm going.'

'How deep is it?'

'Not very. It's fairly shallow in most places and it's not wide, so you'll always be within a few strokes of the bank. You won't come to any harm here, a big strong girl like you.'

Danni gazed wistfully at the water. 'Sure you don't want me?'

He grinned at that. 'Is that a two-edged question?' and Danni riposted crossly,

'No, it isn't. You have a devious mind. I don't need a keeper. I was asking whether you need my assistance with your work.'

Jay shook his head, grinning wickedly. 'No, I don't need you in that way at the moment. There's a rock canyon not far away, with more caves, and our photographs of the Aboriginal paintings were damaged. I'd like to take a few more. It's fairly inaccessible so I'll take the motorcycle.'

'How about Lionel?'

'He's riding pillion with me. We'll be away a couple of hours, maybe a little longer.'

Danni watched Jay depart, camera bag on his back, the small bright-eyed dog on the pillion seat behind him. Lionel barked wistfully when a flock of cockatoos swooped close to the motorcycle, acknowledging their presence with umbrage, but like the well trained animal he was, he did not move from the cushioned seat behind his master.

When they had disappeared from sight Danni collected her costume and changed among the greenery around the pool. It was heaven in the water, almost like a spa bath with the spring water bubbling around her as it tumbled over the logs. She dipped her head underwater, smoothing the long damp hair back from her forehead, letting it stream in the water, feeling incredibly refreshed.

Jay had left her no work to do, she was free. She frolicked in the pool, washed out a few undies, being careful not to contaminate the pool with soap, then looked wistfully again at the refreshing water.

She glanced down at her costume and hesitated. She had a fancy to feel the bubbles brushing against her skin, and on impulse she stripped. A couple of hours Jay had promised to be away, maybe a little longer, and there was nobody else for miles.

It was less than an hour since Jay had left so she had plenty of time for a naked splash. Arranging her costume to dry on the nearest rock, with her towel beside them, Danni let herself down into the water.

A few strokes took her to the fallen logs, and she clung to one of them, bracing herself against the swirling current, delighting in the feeling of freedom and exhilar-

ation. She moved her legs in the water and clung to the
log, long, wet hair trailing.

The eerie feeling began suddenly, as if someone had
turned on a switch. One moment she was splashing
happily in the water, the next her prickling skin and
alerted senses told her everything was not as it should
be.

She dropped deeper into the water, let go the logs, and
allowed the swirling eddies to float her towards the bank.
Then in the shallows she lost power, and floated.

A quick scan of the banks around the pool revealed
nothing unusual. But there *was* something, there had to
be.

Could she have missed hearing the motorcycle return?

It wasn't likely; the swishing water would not have
drowned out the harsh sound of a motorcycle, and there
surely would have been some fluttering and agitation
from the birds around the pool.

Frantically, Danni measured with her eyes the distance to the bank where she had left her bathing suit
and towel. A faint movement in the ferns nearby caught
her attention, just the merest flickering of a shadow, and
she froze.

Then as she narrowed her eyes Danni spied the small
shape of Lionel curled among shading green. Leaves and
shadows made confusing camouflage, but it was Lionel
all right.

And where Lionel lurked, his master would not be far
away. Danni's eyes flashed anger.

'You can come out and show yourself,' she shrieked
furiously towards the screening undergrowth. 'Don't sit
there peeking. I know you're there.'

With horror she heard Jay's answering voice perilously close to where she floated.

'I'm not spying on you. Just getting ready to join you.'
The greenery shook. A pair of shorts landed lightly on

the rock beside Danni's towel. To Danni's instant horror the greenery shook once more and out stepped Jay, as naked as she was.

She turned her head, in a split-second movement, but not before her traitorous senses registered the riveting sight of him, muscled and tanned, full-frontal, strolling calmly to the water's edge.

Danni almost lost control. 'Get away from here,' she ordered shrilly. 'I'm coming out.'

He raised one ironic eyebrow. 'That should be exciting,' and didn't move.

Danni propelled herself close to the bank, keeping carefully submerged, treading water with her back to Jay, accusing over her shoulder,

'You're a cheap snoop, creeping up like that. Don't tell me you rode that bike back here. I'd have heard it.'

'Had a bit of bad luck. Punctured a tyre and had to wheel the last half-mile.' He was lying. Brazenly, insolently, daring her to contradict him. Danni took the bait.

'Puncture be damned,' she snapped. 'You're a nasty devious common cheat. If that's the way you get your kicks, snooping up on people like a prowler, I feel sorry for you.'

Jay looked pointedly at the discarded bathing suit lying beside the towel.

'I didn't ask you to strip,' he drawled. 'You did that all by your sweet self. What for, I wonder?'

'Oh, you make me sick. For heaven's sake get into the water, or go and hide or something, and let me get out and dress. I've had enough of you—you pervert.'

Jay refused to move. He wasn't going to be ruffled. He laughed, and the triumphant undertone of that laughter snapped the last shred of Danni's composure. She lifted her right arm and sent a great splash of water towards the taunting naked man on the bank.

Then she scrambled out, turning her back on him, grabbing her towel, but the man was too quick. He whipped it out of her fingers.

Without stopping to look where she was going Danni bent and scooped up her costume and ran. She was stumbling into a clump of tall sharp reeds when Jay flung himself after her.

'Stand still, you idiot. That stuff is sharp as knives, it'll rip you to pieces.' He dived at her, bringing her down, turning her away from the innocent-looking green growth, his arms holding her tightly against his own body.

The feel of his naked flesh against her own set Danni struggling for freedom. Jay tightened his grip and by sheer force rolled her over and tumbled them both out of the tall spiky reeds.

As he rolled against her Danni curved her fingers into talons. She felt her fingernails digging into naked flesh, ripping Jay's side, and she thought she drew blood. Jay swore but did not lose his grip.

He carried her back to the rock, reached down and deftly picked up the towel he had dropped on the grass, holding Danni with his other arm. Deftly he twisted the towel around her body before releasing her.

'Let's have a look at the damage.'

She wasn't really hurt. Two jagged scratches sliced across her shins setting small trickles of blood meandering down to her ankles. There were a few shallow cuts on her arms, none of them severe.

Jay unwound the towel from her body and pushed her towards the water.

'Get in there and wash the blood off, then we'll put some antiseptic on the scratches.'

He said nothing about his own injuries. Danni caught a glimpse of several cruelly deep scratches on his side.

She had fought better than she expected, but it didn't give her much satisfaction. She was too shaken to gloat.

Jay went to camp for the first-aid kit, pulling on his shorts and striding away without looking back, and when Danni came out of the pool and dressed in her bathing-suit she turned to see him returning with antiseptic and cotton wool.

He swabbed the scratches without comment and when it was done Danni said awkwardly, 'You'd better put some on yourself,' and she was embarrassed to feel the rush of warm blood to her face. He touched one of her hot cheeks lightly.

'That's some temper you've got, lady.'

'And you haven't got anything.' Danni bit the words out furiously, trying to hide the faint trembling of her lips. 'You're nothing but a—a self-opinionated bore with a colossal nerve and a highly inflated opinion of your talents, physical and otherwise.'

That took all her breath. She stood glaring at him, flags of hot colour flying in her cheeks, and she saw the strong jaw clamp tightly, the danger signals glinting in his eyes.

'Don't overdo the indignation, woman. You asked for it, you know.'

Danni choked. 'I didn't ask for anything.' She gulped and sought for more accusations, but the treacherous quivering of her lips stopped the flow of words.

She averted her head quickly, screening her distress. He held her quietly for a moment.

'Calm down.' The hands that picked up the towel and rearranged it around her were unexpectedly gentle. 'You haven't been raped and you aren't going to be. I was only teasing, just seizing on a situation and deciding to develop it for what it was worth. That's what you might call it.'

'That's not what I'd call it. And there wasn't any situation to—to develop.'

'Perhaps not.'

His face softened. He even managed to look faintly apologetic.

'I honestly didn't have anything like this in mind when I went off. We did have a puncture, Lionel and I. Which reminds me, where is the little bloke?'

Lionel still sat among the green ferns. His eyes expressed an urgent desire to join Jay and Danni in whatever game they were playing but Jay had given him the sign to sit, and he would not move until released from the command. Jay snapped his fingers and the dog bounded towards them, barking delightedly.

As he bent to pat the dog, Jay shot Danni a sideways glance. 'Your virtue wasn't really threatened,' he said quietly. 'I sneaked in to watch you enjoying the water—even brought the camera. Then I saw your gear on the bank and realised you were—er—starkers.' He grinned teasingly. 'The rest you know. I guess I went off the beam but I only meant it as a tease. And I'm glad you didn't cut yourself to pieces.'

It could have been an apology. Maybe it was. He said, 'How about you go and rest for a while. I'll have the next best thing to a cold shower and dip myself in the pool. Then I'll cook our meal. Don't start anything. The chores are on me.'

He began to unbutton his shorts again and Danni turned away hurriedly and walked towards the camp. A few seconds later she heard the splash as Jay entered the water, and she was shocked to find in her mind an instant flashback, the picture of his powerful naked body in all its animal splendour imprinted on her memory.

Like some computer gone haywire, her senses kept flashing the full-frontal picture of her family's enemy, Jackson North, standing like some bronzed jungle-man beside the pool, and no matter how desperately she willed the picture away it kept returning to her mind. Jay North, walking towards her, broad-shouldered, lean-hipped, the crisp black curly hair of his body gleaming as he moved in the sunlight.

Gods were made like this man; that was the wayward thought that slipped into her confused emotions, and she pushed it away firmly. Common sense told her that this encounter with Jackson North could be the most dangerous thing that had ever happened to her.

That confidence of his had deadly impact. She lacked the experience to play the kind of games he played, or to fence successfully with his approaches. So she must see he kept his distance and she kept hers until they arrived back at the caravan park.

Be careful, she warned herself, you're on your own with a man who knows how to handle people. He's an expert, a decidedly tricky manipulator, and if you're going to survive you'd better think up a few tricks yourself.

But how did you defend yourself against a man with so much confidence and power and experience?

He certainly knew how to stir up a storm, and storms could be wearing and destructive. They were far from Danni's idea of the perfect environment.

Storms created havoc, and this was certainly no time to start letting a man she hardly knew create havoc with her life.

She would have to be very careful for the remainder of this journey. Jay North didn't have to practise seduction: he was seduction itself.

CHAPTER EIGHT

BACK at camp Danni dressed and flung herself into feverish activity. She was not sure where Jay intended pitching tents but she had to do something, anything, to keep her mind from swinging back to the shock of that scene beside the thermal pool.

She set up stove and gas cylinder, and when Jay came back she was cooking.

'I told you not to do anything.'

Danni didn't look at him. 'I felt like work.'

'Needed to keep busy, did you?'

Danni banged the frying pan down on the stove. 'Don't start misinterpreting everything I do. I'll be glad when this whole project is finished.'

'We may have other business to attend to when we get back.'

She turned then. His face was enigmatic.

'No, we don't. You have nothing more to do at all when this is over except leave Uncle Edwin in his caravan park, and stop harrassing my family.'

Jay wasn't looking at her, but past her, far away in the background as if the distant purple hills might have demanded his attention totally, but he was aware of her.

As she walked past him to collect more cooking-oil his arm lashed out, whip-hard and fast, and his fingers imprisoned her hand, so that she had to pause.

'Don't you want to talk to me?'

'Of course.' Danni kept her tone cool and steady. 'I'll talk to you.' He didn't let her go, and she put distance between them with her voice. 'Where are we headed tomorrow?'

'All right. We'll play it your way.' Now he released her, faint mockery in the half-smile he gave her. 'We should reach a section of the dingo fence. I was planning to stay with one of the boundary riders and his family, but I don't think we'll get that far. We'll set up camp when it gets dark, and I'll take some more film next day, I think.'

Danni knew about the dingo fence, the longest fence in the world she had heard it said, erected to prevent wild dogs and rabbits and other pests from roaming.

Jay said, 'It will probably be hot and dusty but I think you'll find it interesting. *And* informative,' he added, with a tight smile.

He was the boss again, the authority figure, withdrawn and remote, and she was the obedient assistant; but something had happened to them both. The atmosphere of casual contact that had built up between them over the last few days was gone.

Danni sensed it in Jay and she felt it strongly in herself, a tension ready to crack at the slightest hint of confrontation.

And still he didn't trust her, Danni was sure of it. As they cleared away after their evening meal she caught him watching her, eyes faintly narrowed, as if he might have suspected that she had engineered that situation at the pool.

Next morning Jay stayed carefully casual, offering antiseptic for her scratches, urging her to keep them clean although they were only superficial.

Danni dared not mention the marks she had gouged on his side, the angry red marks she remembered vividly on an otherwise perfect body.

But there was awkwardness between them, a constraint only partly relaxed when they stopped for lunch and Lionel enjoyed himself chasing a large grey kangaroo.

The huge beast did not appear alarmed, merely loping away with slow scornful bounds as if its dignity demanded a respite from the small yapping animal at its heels. Lionel returned, shaking his head, sitting with expectant bright eyes as he awaited approval for what he no doubt considered a victory.

It was late afternoon when they reached the dingo fence, after ploughing over countless sandhills, and Danni got out and opened the gate for Jay to drive through, waiting to shut it carefully as they turned on to a dirt track, only too well aware of the printed sign telling her the heavy penalties in fines for anybody failing to close the gate securely.

Jay pulled up alongside a deserted shack. 'Not exactly the Ritz, but it'll have to do. One of the fence-maintenance riders used it until he married and they built him a larger house. We'll take advantage of it tonight instead of putting up our tents on the cold sand. That is, if you don't mind.'

Danni wasn't going to say she minded, she knew that nights in the desert could be bitterly cold. She explored the old building dubiously. There were cracks between the timbers in some of the walls but it would certainly provide better shelter than their tents. There were two bunks in the sleeping quarters, and a table against the wall just inside the door.

They ate their evening meal, and later that evening were carrying their equipment into the old building when Jay glanced obliquely at Danni's legs.

'Looks as if we've left our marks on each other, doesn't it?' he queried softly, and Danni flushed.

'No credit to you,' she countered.

'No, I realise that.' Jay was lighting the lamp. He put it down on the table and walked to Danni, curving his long fingers around her chin, tilting her face towards his.

'I've apologised, I think. If I didn't, I meant to, and if I did I'm not sure it got through, anyway. I was out of order yesterday and I'm sorry I upset you.'

Jackson North wasn't a man of apologies. That little speech must have been difficult. Danni's mouth softened.

'Yes, you have. Apologised, I mean. And I'm sorry too. I didn't mean to carry on an everlasting grudge—and I——' she sighed deeply '—I suppose it could be called asking for trouble if I decide to go nude-bathing when there's a cameraman around.'

'Rubbish.' Jay was testing the strength of the top bunk, rapping the timbers to make sure they were sound. 'You had every right to expect privacy at the pool, and next time you shall have it. Now we'd better bring in the rest of our belongings and go to bed.'

He seemed unusually mellow tonight. As they walked outside into the darkness he offered, 'Look up at the stars, Danni. It could be a long time before you see another sky as spectacular as this one.'

He was right. Out in the desert the stars seemed almost unreal, larger than life, hanging low and glittering, setting the sky alive.

Danni looked up at them as she walked along, amusing herself with the star-patterns, when the silence was split wide open by a blood-curdling howl. She gasped.

'Dingo,' Jay said tersely. 'Don't let him worry you. He won't get you.'

But he moved closer, shepherding her to the four-wheel-drive, opening up and pulling out the two rolled sleeping-bags and a few blankets as extra cover.

'It'll probably be a cold night,' he explained unnecessarily.

He collected the rest of their gear and slammed the door shut, and he was bending to pick up the blankets when the dingo howled again, this time longer and louder and even more blood-curdling, and Danni shuddered and put her hands over her ears to shut out the dismal sound.

'Haven't you heard the wild dogs howl before?' Jay sounded faintly amused but Danni couldn't disguise her reaction.

'I know it's ridiculous but it sounds so gruesome. Like witch's night in the haunted cave. Spooks and hauntings '

'Danni, you're out of this world.' Jay dropped the sleeping-bags and the blankets and he was laughing, almost hatefully, until suddenly all in a moment he was not laughing any more.

He put his arms around her shoulders and he said half seriously, 'That's wonderful. I thought you didn't have a weakness. You'll have to control that imagination. It's wild.'

His grip was comforting and Danni mumbled, 'I'm sorry. I really am. I must be tired. I don't think I'm neurotic. At least, I hope not, but I didn't expect to hear anything and it spooked me.'

'Of course you aren't, you foolish female. I must admit, it's an eerie sound those wild creatures make, when you hear it for the first time. I ought to let you off work tomorrow. I've been pushing too hard.'

Danni leaned her head against his shoulder and suddenly all her fears were ridiculous. Dingo howls, personal confrontations, unknown futures—what did they matter if you felt secure, and she felt secure enough now with Jay's strong arms around her. She could handle them all.

She lifted her face and smiled at him. He said her name softly, and tightened his arm around her, and then he began stroking her throat and neck from jawline to the sensitive hollow at the base of her neck, trailing his fingers in a feathering arousal that set her pulses racing.

His hips pressed against hers, turning the whole of her body into one trembling and urgent desire, and he moved slowly in gentle stimulation until desire flared into passion, and she was grasping at him with hungry, clinging fingers, lifting her lips towards his, beseeching him . . .

He murmured something softly, an inarticulate sound ending in a groan, before he swung her body around and took her in his arms, and put her down gently where the blankets lay strewn on the sand. He dropped beside her, crouching, his face very close to hers.

'Danni?' It was a question, not a demand. It meant, Are you sure, and Are you ready for me? and Danni held up her arms and curved them lovingly around his neck, pulling him slowly down until he lay, warm and urgent with need, beside her. He slid one hand between the buttons of her cotton shirt.

'Danni, you do to me what no other woman has ever done and you do it so easily. Without even trying, you drive me to distraction. Just a look from those mysterious green eyes, or the way you move your hips, even the sound of your voice—even your anger. That's all it takes, and I'm yours.'

'Do you really mean that?'

He nodded in the starlight. 'Sometimes I feel I've always known you would come along some wonderful day and ruin my peace of mind. I think I even dreamed about you. Certainly I remembered after that day in the studio——'

Dreamily Danni traced the shape of his lips, softened now in sensuality, with her fingertip.

'I wish I'd dreamed about you. It might have been fun.'

He kissed her finger lightly, then moved his head to rest his cheek against the softness of her hair, groaning into its silken waves.

'Fun, she calls it. Danni, I ache for you. If you pulled away—if you got up and left me now—if you walked away from me—I think some part of me would die. I'm sure of it.'

'I'm not going anywhere, I'm staying here.' Danni pressed her slim body against his. She was committed now. Over his shoulder she saw the low-hanging stars glittering on the horizon, and she repeated softly, 'I don't have any plans to go anywhere. That's a promise,' but even as she said the words she knew they weren't true. She was certainly going somewhere, she was heading for the stars, and she was going to reach that tantalising glitter because Jay was going to take her there.

Hadn't she known from the first touch of his fingers that tonight had to be the night, the turning-point in her life?

Not without shyness Danni slid her hand under his shirt, then, feeling Jay's immediate response, she lost all hesitation and tightened her grasp, feeling quite sure that for Jay too this was going to be some kind of special experience.

The quickened beating of his heart, the urgent breath on her cheek, told her of his total abandonment to the contact.

This was going to be a high for them both. To every caress and every touch of Jay's fingers Danni responded with an instinctive reaction of her own, and when the wonderful consummation happened they were both out of this world, swinging towards the stars, up into the silence and the promise, swept away by powerful sensations that were new to Danni, and she let them carry her into another dimension of life, one that was exhilarating and exciting and satisfying beyond description.

Afterwards they lay quietly, body against body, arms wrapped around each other, until Jay moved reluctantly.

'I wish we could stay here all night but we'd better get you inside. Can't have you catching your death when the cold comes down.'

Somewhere in that feverish and beautiful lovemaking they had shed their clothes. Danni reached for hers but Jay took them out of her hands.

'Let me do that.'

He began dressing her tenderly, but before it was finished he admitted wryly, 'You'd better finish this. I'm not as strong as I thought I was.'

He turned away, pulling on his own discarded clothing, gathering up the sleeping-bags and blankets and the rest of the equipment.

Somewhere out in the blackness a dingo howled but Danni scarcely noticed.

Jay put one arm over her shoulders and steered her slowly towards the old house, and she walked in a fantasy world of shadows and sky and sand and stars.

As they walked under the derelict veranda Jay glanced up at the starry sky.

'Sorry we didn't get high enough to grab you one of those silver things. Perhaps we'll make it another time.'

The words were like a piercing cold wind blowing across Danni's happiness. Jay hadn't reached the stars... Could that be what he was telling her?

Of course we reached them, she told herself fervently. I did, anyway. But perhaps it was not quite like that for Jay.

As they walked into the house he looked at her oddly, as if he might have been waiting for her to say something.

She could have told him, You were wrong about the stars. I went way up past them. But something stopped her. Suppose it hadn't been such a remarkable experience for him? Suppose her extravagant fancy merely amused him?

Danni gave a little shiver, knowing she couldn't bear it if that should happen.

She managed to say lightly, 'We certainly don't seem to have jolted any of the constellations out of their courses. Everything seems to be going on up there exactly as before,' and he looked at her quickly before he stacked the sleeping-bags on the bunks.

'I'll take the top one, since my legs are longer than yours,' he offered quietly. 'Sleep well, Danni, and don't be too disappointed. I'll get you a star some day.'

But Danni knew she was not disappointed. She had abandoned pride and self-control and she had walked into that experience knowing exactly what she was doing.

She bent to push her suitcase under the bunk, turning her face from him, afraid he might see the betraying rush of colour into her cheeks, but he moved so that he stood directly behind her as she straightened. He slid his long arms around her, crossing them so that each open palm cupped a breast, and Danni's senses surged again.

'Was it good for you, Danni?'

Foolish to deny it. It must have showed. She nodded without speaking.

'For both of us,' he affirmed, bending to kiss the pulse on her neck, letting her feel the warmth of lips and tongue as he teased her a little before moving away.

'Dream of me,' he suggested, eyebrows quizzical as he prepared to climb into the upper bunk.

'Maybe.'

She waited until Jay had settled down before she relaxed. There was pleasure in her body, and pain in her heart. It had been good for Jay but he hadn't reached the stars. Not tonight.

Was he warning her not to place too much importance on what had happened between them? She huddled into the warmth of her sleeping-bag, wrapping her own arms around her body to keep out the cold, wondering what tomorrow would bring.

As they got ready to drive away from the fence next day Danni looked back at the old house wistfully. Jay had spent most of the morning miles away photographing a grader at work as it freed a section of the fence from drifts of shifting sand. Now they were ready to move away and Danni knew she would probably never see again the small timber building with all the memories it held for her.

She knew she had experienced a watershed in her life. Whatever happened from here on, she would never again be the rather naïve Danielle Paige who had allowed herself to be persuaded—no, blackmailed—into this journey.

She was a woman now, a person who had made an important choice that would alter from here on the way she looked at life and the values she placed on situations.

Jay was rolling up the sleeves of his checked shirt. He said softly, 'OK?' and Danni nodded.

'That's a good girl.'

He gave her an approving look, a definitely masculine glance of power, and Danni bridled. 'What does that mean?'

His eyes sharpened. He took a minute to shape his reply.

'It means,' he said deliberately, 'I like a lady who can make up her own mind, and I have never met anyone who could send me up in flames quite so devastatingly as you did last night. In other words, Danielle, thank you for a remarkable experience, and I look forward to more.'

Danni's hackles were still rising.

'I hope you're not being a male chauvinist——'

He turned on her swiftly. 'Now it's my turn. Just exactly what does that mean?'

Danni sighed. 'I don't know—not precisely. It's not that I'm having doubts or regrets.' She flushed self-consciously. 'I went up in flames, too. But I don't like to be patted on the head and told I'm a good girl.'

'Heaven help us!' He rolled his eyes and pushed her towards the passenger seat, and when he sat beside her and started up the motor Danni took one last look over her shoulder at what they were leaving behind, and she said to herself, in her innermost thoughts, I wish you would say something like I love you, or even I think I love you.

And if that's too much to ask, I would appreciate something like a statement of intent... Am I just another experience for you, a pleasure-venture that you hope to repeat a couple of times more before you go on to somebody else?

If only she dared ask him just how many of those murmured endearments he had really meant. Perhaps she could ask him, Would it really shatter you if I walked away?

He had said, 'You drive me to distraction, and you ruin my peace of mind.' His peace of mind looked quite intact today.

As they topped their first sandhill Jay turned and flashed her a warm, lazy smile, as if he guessed the tenor of her wayward thoughts, and wanted to reassure her. Then he settled down to driving, and Danni checked the script of their next assignment.

They were headed for an abandoned mining settlement. They would not stay long, Jay briefed her—all he wanted was to photograph the ghost-town location as it was now, with the mine closed and most of the houses sold and re-located, the surrounding streets and gardens left to nature.

Danni expected to find a desolate and deserted air hanging over the abandoned settlement, but trees and flowers and creeping vines in many of the gardens still flourished, and there was an atmosphere of pleasant green and vivid colour. This was not a dead town, just a small township asleep in the sunshine.

Poinsettia trees flamed with scarlet star-flowers, camphor laurels and mango trees spread their branches, and the birds sang. One of the few remaining houses had been loaded on to a low-loader and stood waiting, ready to be carted away.

Paradise uninhabited, was Danni's first response as they pulled up alongside what had once been an access road.

Jay took his pictures, dictated a few comments, and they ate lunch among shady trees, sipping cool drinks, listening to the birds.

'It's beautiful still,' Danni said dreamily. 'I only hope the bushland doesn't swallow up the gardens, but I suppose it will in time. I'd like to go for a walk, if there is time.'

'Watch out for venomous snakes.'

'Now you've destroyed the illusion.'

'No.' Jay's comment was dry. 'What I'm doing, Danielle, is reminding you that even in Eden there was a serpent. So watch where you go walking, especially in the long grass.'

Certainly the day was hot enough to bring out any lurking reptiles, and Danni carefully skirted patches of long dry grass as she walked around the outer areas of the settlement.

She wondered whether Jay's dry comment was supposed to carry a message. Could he be sending her a warning that last night's experience might have a dark side? That she was not to regard it as carrying a promise of 'happy-ever-after' stuff?

She tossed a broken branch and Lionel chased it. He looked at her reproachfully. He was a rather small dog, it was a very large branch. She picked up a smaller piece of wood and he retrieved it, tail wagging as he dropped it at her feet.

Maybe another message there, perhaps, if you believed in omens. She had been 'thinking big'—too big?— and a small cold ache was born.

When they drove away Jay went on being casual and friendly, a little more relaxed than usual. Perhaps that was his normal reaction after conquest. He leaned back in the driving-seat and stretched his left arm negligently along the seat behind Danni. He didn't touch her, and later when they entered rougher terrain he took his arm away to concentrate on the difficult driving.

They camped for the night on the edge of a large saucer-shaped depression almost surrounded by a circle of weird rock formations. The only vegetation above ground level was a few scattered clumps of wispy grass, and the wind-smoothed rockpoints thrust their peaks against the darkening sky like the horned backbones of prehistoric animals.

Jay drove up to the only clump of trees that looked leafy enough to offer shelter. 'Can you get us something to eat while I do a bit of investigation? We missed these outcrops on our last trips. There is supposed to be a string of caves with Aboriginal paintings just below that long overhanging ledge. I'll have a look and see if there's anything worth following up in the morning.'

'How long will you be?'

'About half an hour. You get the meal ready. I'll fix the tents before I go.'

Jay was gone a long time. Danni fed Lionel, then busied herself getting the meal. The sky darkened. Danni lit the two gas lamps they carried, vaguely uneasy that Jay might have lost direction. She placed the lights well clear of the trees so that he would be able to see them from a distance, then she sat in the Range Rover, feeling the cold come down, wondering what she ought to do.

Jay had taught her how to use the radios. She could get in touch with the Flying Doctor Service or one of the homesteads in an emergency. But how was she to know whether this was an emergency or whether Jay was merely taking longer than he expected?

Lionel, curled beside her, gave a little whimper and snuggled closer. Restlessly Danni gathered him in her arms, opened the door and stepped outside. She held the dog close to her face.

'Can you find him for me, Lion? Can you find Jay?' Gently she put him down, and he whimpered again, turned around as if seeking direction, then looked up at her doubtfully.

'I guess that's asking too much. I'll come with you. We'll walk in the direction he went and we'd better make some noise. I'll shout until he answers.'

But she did not have to shout. She was buttoning up her jacket against the cool air when Jay's dark form stumbled around the trees and he came into the light of the nearest lamp.

'Took longer than I thought,' he said calmly, then crumpled down at her feet in a dead faint.

As she bent over him Danni saw first that his shirt was torn and there were scratches on his hands and legs. Then she moved the lamp and the pallor of his face frightened her. He was not bleeding but an enormous bump on his forehead showed swollen and faintly purple and there were small brown burrs from the dry grasses clinging to his hair.

Danni moved him cautiously, covering him with blankets, cupping his head with her hand as she slid a cushion under it. Unexpectedly he opened his eyes, the eyelids flickering in his grey-white face.

'I'm all right.' His smile was crooked. 'I may not look it, but I really am OK. Just took a tumble, that's all.'

'You could have concussion. What should I do?' She didn't think he was going to answer, and was almost ready to send out a radio message for help when he spoke.

'Brandy. A good strong dose,' and his voice was stronger.

Danni poured the brandy, holding the glass to his lips with one hand, supporting his head with the other, and thankfully she watched the pallor fade and colour come back into his cheeks. He raised a hand and touched the lump on his forehead gingerly.

'Oh boy, what a headache. As you've probably gathered I didn't make it safely down from the caves. I had a fall.'

'Yes.'

'Damn fool thing to do.' He moved his legs, then raised himself to a sitting position. 'I promise not to do it again.'

'I wish you'd lie down. Suppose you do have concussion?'

'I don't believe I have. There's no nausea, just this damn-nuisance headache.' He held out the glass for a refill of brandy. 'Let it go till morning. I'll let you help me to my tent in a couple of minutes.'

'Shouldn't you have some attention?'

'There's healing-cream in the first-aid kit, that will reduce the swelling on my forehead, and I'll let you have the pleasure of dabbing antiseptic on my scratches when I've settled down. After that,' he grinned apologetically, 'I'll probably sleep all night.'

He watched faintly amused while Danni checked his pulse-rate, holding his wrist. 'Shall I live?'

'All right so far, but if you start acting strangely in the night where's the nearest doctor? Do I radio or drive?'

'Don't worry. There's a sizeable town not too far away from here, in the direction we were heading when we turned off. If I get worse you can drive me to a doctor there. Meanwhile if you don't mind, how about tucking me into my tent?'

Danni made Jay as comfortable as she could. He even managed to eat a little food and swallow a large mug of tea, black and well sweetened, before he lay back and drifted off to sleep.

For Danni there would be no sleep. She lay on her own sleeping-bag squeezed beside Jay in his tent, and Lionel curled at her feet, as if he understood this was a time when she needed companionship.

Several times Jay stirred, and Danni leaned her head on her hand, watching until he settled again. Once he lifted his hand to touch the dressing on his forehead and Danni, fearful that he might dislodge it, curled her fingers around his wrist and gently guided his arm down and away from the injury.

In the dim light she saw him turn his head. His eyes opened and he stared at her, while his lips moved.

Danni bent to listen. At first the whispered syllables escaped her, then he repeated them, 'Eleanor... Eleanor...' His lips curved in a smile of loving gentleness, then he gave a long steady sigh, a sigh of pure happiness, and closed his eyes. Danni sank back on to her own sleeping-bag, trying not to believe what she had just heard but knowing it was true, and her whole world was tumbling into ruins.

He had looked at her in the dim light and imagined her to be somebody else. Somebody he loved. Eleanor. Who was Eleanor?

Her heart aching, eyes filling with silent tears, Danni lay blinking at the wall of the tent, and when morning came there were dark shadows under her eyes, and unspeakable pain in her heart.

CHAPTER NINE

IN the morning Jay's breathing was regular and he showed no sign of fever, and Danni eased herself slowly out of his tent, being careful not to disturb him as she washed, dressed and prepared breakfast.

Jay was out of bed before the meal was ready, but Danni didn't even try to produce the smile he obviously expected as he blew her a light kiss. Some sensitive part of her had been destroyed last night, a foolish over-trusting remnant of a naïve girl who had set out on this journey. Never again would she rush headlong into an experience, no matter how enticing.

There would be no more overdone imaginings about reaching for the stars. Every sane person had accepted long ago that the stars were out of reach. Nobody could afford to believe otherwise. You didn't do yourself any favours that way.

She looked at Jay and asked, 'How many eggs for breakfast?' and the stilted way she spoke sounded off balance, even to her own ears, but there was nothing she could do about it.

All she wanted now was a fence between herself and the man who had made a fool of her, using her so easily for his own entertainment.

'I never knew a woman with your magic,' he had told her and that was only one of the extravagant things he had said.

And she had swallowed every false word, lapped up every outrageous compliment, like a love-starved child.

155

Jay glanced at her quickly as she handed him his breakfast but said nothing. He dressed the wound on his forehead and treated the scratches himself, and when they had packed up he whistled for Lionel and they drove off without taking the photographs he had intended. Apparently the caves had proved disappointing.

He let Danni do the driving.

She asked distantly, 'Should I take you to a doctor?' and he answered tersely, 'No, thanks.' He was getting the message all right.

They wasted little time on meals that day. Jay continued to brush away talk about his fall and injury but he must have been stiff and hurting because he moved awkwardly, and there was weariness in his face, so Danni drove all day.

He insisted on helping set up camp that evening, and when they were ready for sleep they settled in the shelter of an old shed and windmill, and just when she thought he had settled down for the night Jay came to her tent.

'Would you feel better if I kissed you goodnight?'

Danni didn't answer. She couldn't. But still Jay lingered.

'I asked you——'

'No!' To Danni, her own voice sounded like an agonised whisper.

'I could change your mind.' He didn't understand. He thought she was concerned with his injuries. 'Don't worry. It won't hurt me. I'm not that bruised.'

He slipped quickly into her tent, unzipping the long slide fastening of her sleeping-bag, easing himself beside her.

'No!'

'Yes,' he contradicted. In the darkness she felt rather than saw his confident smile, and as she raised herself to push him away he pressed down on her shoulders, and moved part of his body-weight over hers.

'Lie down,' he ordered. 'Lie down and love me. I need you desperately, Danielle.'

Did he? Certainly his lips spoke of need. They pressed hard against hers with feverish intensity, and if the sensations that contact aroused in him were anything like her own response, then right at this moment Jay probably did need her.

A shaft of pain stabbed through Danni's emotions as a calm reasonable inward voice asked her, For how long?

She pushed it away, softening her lips so that Jay deepened the kissing into passionate arousal, and soon her whole body throbbed in overpowering response.

Jay's hands moved swiftly over her skin, lighting fires, exciting every cell with his ardent touching until she was ready once again to do anything he asked.

She heard herself uttering small inarticulate sounds, deep in her throat, and Jay answering with a series of incoherent pleasure-sounds that sent her senses reeling.

She kissed him feverishly and rejoiced in the long shudder of delight that shook his body. He was reaching for the knotted straps of her cotton nightdress when sanity came to Danni in one sharp clear flash. Whatever was she doing?

He didn't love her. He loved Eleanor. Desperately, she pushed him away, dragging the sleeping-bag around her, curling herself so that his desperate hands could not reach her.

'Danni!' His voice was husky, almost pleading.

'Go away.'

At first he didn't believe it. Then as she tensed her muscles and tightened her grip of the protective sleeping-bag, he accepted her decision with a muttered oath.

'That's what I like,' he said bitterly. 'A woman who knows what she wants.' His lips were tight with disdain. 'I hope it amused you, lady, to have me half out of my mind. What was it for? Did your ego need a boost?'

Furiously he charged out of the tent. Danni heard twigs and dry leaves crackling under his feet as he headed for his own sleeping place. Even then she didn't relax.

The ache in her heart was a mixture of lost pleasure and self-inflicted pain. She should never have let him in. She didn't want to be just another experience, not with this man.

He doesn't love me, she told herself again. He never pretended to love me.

She wondered dully whether he had been seeking to mark up another conquest, or while away the time, or whether perhaps his approaches had masked something darker and more sinister. Uncle Edwin had said, 'There is a streak of madness in the North family. He wants revenge. The opal wasn't enough.'

Perhaps the humiliation of Ryan Paige's daughter would have been another notch in his gun, another small triumph to balance against the imagined hurt of something that had happened all those years ago.

As she waited desperately for sleep, Danni heard the mournful wail of a night-bird, and she knew that when this journey was over that was what she would remember—the long sad mourning of night creatures in bushland and desert and the flat red plains, and the answering loneliness in her own heart.

Jackson North she would try not to remember. He would be free to go to his island, she to her uncle's caravan park, when they got back home. And he could find his Eleanor.

The name stabbed her like a swift infliction of pain that set tears springing behind her eyes.

Eleanor. How he must love her, whoever she was. That look of tenderness on his face had been a complete transformation.

If I ever meet her, Danni told herself fiercely, I'll probably want to kill her. This was a sensation new to her, the stabbing jealous pain, the longing to be the only one desired and loved, the important one, to have Jay murmur her name and not Eleanor's if he ever again drifted through clouds of pain.

Go to sleep, she told herself fiercely, go to sleep; and she did eventually, though it wasn't easy.

Next morning Jay took over some of the driving. Danni sat rigidly beside him, and when he allowed her to take a spell at the wheel later he leaned back in his seat quietly, occasionally passing some stilted remark about the scenery they were passing through.

Danni answered him in the same kind of voice, her heart and her throat aching, and after a while he lapsed into silence, his expression weary, and Danni was too miserable to care.

She had been an idiot, over-enthusiastic about a dalliance that must have been an everyday occurrence for the great Jackson North.

Bitterly Danni faced the truth, telling herself, If I were more sophisticated I could laugh this off. I could chatter brightly, close my heart against him, keep my pride.

But I can't do that, not yet anyway. Maybe later when I am home with my family, doing familiar things, chatting up customers in the shop...

It all seemed so far away she found a sudden blurring of tears in her eyes, and Jay shot out a strong arm and grabbed the steering-wheel as they narrowly missed a culvert beside the road.

'I'll take over now,' he said curtly. He had always been able to tune in to her thinking. He knew she was switched off, and turned away from him. Whatever had happened between them was all over, finished before it had really begun.

Danni settled in the passenger seat until they crossed the mountains and the landscape changed again, this time less stark, although inside the four-wheel-drive things could not have been colder or sharper.

When Jay turned off the main road on to a dirt track and stopped before a five-barred gate he said coolly,

'If you don't mind,' and Danni alighted, opened the gate and fastened it shut after Jay had driven through.

There were cattle scattered in the paddocks. They stood in the sunlight grazing, flicking their tails at the flies.

There were two more gates to open, two more paddocks to cross, and when they finally stopped Danni swallowed unhappily and said,

'You didn't give me a script.'

'There's no script for this.' Jay's tone was sombre. They were pulled up alongside a broken-down picket fence that had once obviously contained a large garden, and Jay pushed aside twisted branches of dead trees as he stepped over fallen pickets, and they walked through the dead depressing garden through tangled high grasses that tugged at Danni's cotton slacks.

She followed Jay with trepidation. Something in his grim expression, the forbidding set of his jaw and the impatience with which he pushed aside the dead growth made Danni feel a stirring of expectation, a premonition of disaster.

Jay knew where he was going. Never once did he stop and look around him for direction, even when they crossed the weedy remains of what had once been a gravel driveway.

Overgrown with wild grasses now it still held enough gravel to crunch underfoot, and they walked along it to the top of a small rise.

On the hillside stood a derelict house—no, a homestead, Danni corrected herself. This had once been no ordinary home. It must have been a mansion, double-storeyed with pitched roof and many gables, but it was old and neglected now.

Jay pushed open the front door and dust fell from somewhere above, and Danni gasped, because the inside of the homestead was an empty shell. She moved to walk through the doorway but Jay rasped, 'Keep out. It's dangerous,' and pushed her away.

He stood there for what seemed to Danni an interminable time, staring around him, and Danni had the feeling that if she spoke he would not have heard her.

Then suddenly his lips tightened, his features hardened, and he dragged the door shut again.

As they walked down the broken stone steps they had to dodge an ancient tree that thrust one bare branch across their path. A frangipani, gnarled and leafless, yet with one solitary flower clinging to the twisted branch as if it had fallen there from another world where things lived, and not this dreadful place where everything had died.

Jay reached out a hand and snapped off the branch.

'Oh, no!' Danni could not bite back the protest as he crumpled the flower in his fingers and dropped it on to the gravel.

'This is no place for flowers,' he said savagely.

Danni looked over her shoulder at the dying house and shivered.

'It's terrible. Whatever happened? Do you know?'

'Yes, I know. The owners lost all their money after five years of drought, and had to sell it for a song.'

'Why is it derelict? Didn't the new owner want to live in it?'

'The new owner,' Jay pronounced bitterly, 'was a pastoral company who chose to combine this land with the adjoining property. They already had a manager in one homestead so of course they didn't need another.'

He was walking away from her. 'There used to be a rose garden around here, complete with sundial.'

There were no roses now. Tall grass almost hid the old sundial. Jay ripped grassheads away and stood gazing down at the faded markings on the sundial before he turned his head deliberately to stare at the empty shell of the homestead.

'That was my grandfather's house,' he said. 'And then my father's.'

Before she could stop herself Danni muttered, 'Oh, my God.'

Then with terrible cold insight she added, 'Is this—this what you blame my family for?'

He let her see his face then, hard, unforgiving and accusing.

'When my father was a young married man this district had a long run of dry years, the worst drought this part of the country ever experienced. My father set out with friends—he thought they were friends—to try and retrieve the family fortunes. With the two Paige brothers, your father and your uncle, he went mining for opals, and after a lot of hard slogging and patient digging they found opals. Good stones, of great value.

'My father trusted the Paige brothers to take the stones to a buyer in Coober Pedy, to have them assessed and to sell if the price was right.

'They came back to the claim empty-handed. No opals, no money. Just a cock-and-bull story about the stones having been lost or stolen. He never believed them.'

'Neither do you,' Danni said woodenly. Jay didn't say she was right, but it showed clearly in his face, and when he went to stride away from her Danni put herself in front of him and forced him to look at her.

'My father was an honest man. He would never have stolen from anybody. He would not cheat.'

'Then where are the opals?' His eyes were cold and grey. They looked through her. Danni drew a deep breath.

'You should know. Your father took the opal jewellery that should have been my mother's. He didn't go home empty-handed. I bet you know where it is.'

Her voice was high, almost hysterical, and for several terrible seconds Danni thought Jay was going to strike her.

His lips tightened into a furious line, the muscles on his strong neck stood out like whipcord, and Danni flinched inwardly, half expecting retaliation for her wild accusation.

But she stood her ground, blocking North's way with her own body, her head tilted back and her eyes defiant.

It was only afterwards when Jay made an angry sound in his throat and pushed his way around her, only then did she look down to find her own hands were clenched, the fingernails cutting tiny curves of red into the flesh of her palms, so great had been the tension between them.

She hurried after him, fearful that he might do something drastic like driving away in his fury and leaving her here in this desolate place.

As Jay got into the driver's seat Danni scrambled in on the passenger side and Lionel curled between them. That said it all, she decided bitterly. She and Jackson North were so far apart there had to be something visible between them.

What was it he had said? Yesterday's enemy, tomorrow's lover. But it wasn't true. Yesterday's enemy would always remain just that—the enemy.

As they headed for the road Danni climbed out and opened and shut gates like a robot, with her heart full of tears, and only pride to hold her back from admitting aloud that she was wrong, that she shouldn't have mentioned the necklace and brooch, not at this moment which was so bitter for Jay.

After all, what could it matter now that this one stone had been mislaid somewhere in the skirmishing of families and the desperate search for fortunes? Those small pieces of jewellery could not have been valuable enough to make any difference to the final outcome.

But perhaps it wasn't the lost jewellery that made her cry out so bitterly against Jay's allegations. Pride in her father could have something to do with it, but wasn't it really that she had lashed out at him because he had taken her love and misused it?

They were driving back towards the coast now and Danni found herself thinking gratefully, Oh, but I shall be glad to see my family again.

She found herself watching Jay's stern profile, averting her eyes when they became bemused by the tendrils of dark curls that touched his neck, or the negligent hip-movements as he stretched his legs occasionally to keep away travel weariness.

Danni took her turn at driving, but it was worse then because she felt him watching her in his turn, and her over-responsive senses made her self-conscious and awkward.

He reached for a book, resting one hand on Lionel's rough coat as he began to read, and Danni felt the touch of those fingers as keenly as if they were tangled in her own hair.

When they got to the first coastal town Jay made several phone calls. He rang the caravan park to let Lilyan know they were on their way, and with that call Danni felt the last page was turning in this particular book of experience.

They drove north through Rockhampton and Jay pulled up in the shopping centre. He walked into one of the local bank buildings and when he came out Danni saw he carried a package and a large envelope but he drove on without making any comment, and an hour later they turned into the caravan park and Danni's journey ended.

Danni kissed her mother and received Gregg's boisterous welcome. Her uncle was nowhere to be seen and the ironic lift of Jay's eyebrows told Danni he registered the lack of welcome from Edwin Paige.

He accepted a light meal and two cups of coffee while Lionel watched the birds on the lagoon.

Danni had asked to keep some pages of the script for re-typing, preferring to neaten the final draft, and Jay agreed indifferently.

He seemed in a hurry to leave, explaining to Lilyan and Gregg that he had to return down south to Rockhampton where he would leave the Range Rover and some equipment.

He handed Lilyan the large envelope before he left.

'That will cover the caravan park for the next three years,' he told her, and she thanked him steadily, as if she had expected it.

'I'll be on the island tomorrow. I'll call and pick up the script in a few days' time.' He was talking to Danni but he wasn't really looking at her.

She mumbled, 'I can post it——' and he snapped, 'Don't be ridiculous.'

But this was her day for being ridiculous. She watched Lionel climb on to the passenger seat beside Jay and felt depressed because she had begun to think of it as 'her' seat, and that was about as ridiculous as anyone could get. She would probably never sit there again.

As he moved away Jay leaned out of the window. 'Since this means so much to you, you'd better have it.' It was the parcel he'd collected from the bank.

Danni kept the polite smile pasted on her face until he disappeared, then she went to the caravan to unpack, and she had almost everything back in the wardrobe when Gregg rapped on the door.

'Anything for the washing-machines?'

She handed a plastic bag of her soiled and wrinkled clothes to her brother and she said, 'Thanks. That's one job I won't have to do for myself.'

He was looking at her shrewdly.

'Didn't you enjoy it, sister dear?'

'Yes, I did. Really I did. I've seen lots of places and I'll tell you about some of them tomorrow. Only we've had a long drive and I'm feeling my age.'

'Ha!' Gregg was unimpressed. 'The whole twenty-two years. How sad for you.'

When he was gone Danni picked up Jay's package. Instinct told her what it might contain and she was not at all surprised when she undid the clasp and found an opal brooch, blue-green with swirls of red fire, shaped like a bird with outspread wings. It was very beautiful. The necklace was a gold chain holding a tiny collection of opal chips, probably what remained after the shaping of the bird.

Obviously it was a very small stone, not valuable enough to save even the rose garden of that once-splendid homestead Jay had shown her, but it had been her father's, and she ought to have been thrilled to have it back, but it did not mean anything at all except that her mother might be pleased to see it.

She closed the case and pushed it away at the back of a drawer. She didn't want to touch it, or wear it, and she certainly didn't want to talk about it. Not yet...

Next day Danni completed the re-typing. She worked in the office, ready to serve behind the counter or direct tourists to caravan sites, because her absence had meant Lilyan and Gregg and Uncle Ed sharing her work between them, and she wanted to make up for that.

Later she stapled the scripts and sealed them in a large envelope and across the front she wrote his name 'Jackson North' in clear sharp writing. Then she stowed the envelope on a shelf behind the counter so that he would see it when he called.

She hoped she wasn't around when that happened. It wouldn't help her spirits any to see his dynamic figure stride into the reception area, pick up the envelope, and walk away again. Goodbyes should only be said once. Danni didn't think she could face another one.

She wondered whether Eleanor had waited for Jay out on his island, and the possibility hurt her so much she went quickly to the caravan and pulled the jewel-case out of the drawer and almost ran with it back to the office.

It was nearly lunchtime and Uncle Edwin, her mother and Gregg were all in the office, and Danni put the case down on the counter, the lid open, so they could all see the opals. She had expected her mother to be pleased and elated but Lilyan stood staring at it with such a strange and troubled expression that Danni felt bewildered.

Edwin had no misgivings. 'So he's returned it. And about time, too.'

His plump rosy face registered instant pleasure. He pursed his lips, while Gregg gave a soundless whistle and picked up the brooch, moving it under the light to set the colours glinting. He turned a puzzled face to Danni.

'What's this for? A bonus? Have you been a good girl?'

Uncle Ed shook his head knowingly. 'That's not it at all, young man. This was—is—your mother's, the very first little bit of stone your father dug at Coober Pedy. Now it's been given back, as it should have been years ago.'

'How did Dad lose it?' Gregg scented a story and Edwin obliged.

'Like I said, it was stolen. It's a shabby story, but if you want to hear it——'

'Of course we do.' Gregg forgot lunch, and Edwin Paige launched into a long speech, enjoying the telling, sure everyone was listening. It was a convincing story, but it wasn't long before Danni realised it was not the same version of what had happened at Coober Pedy all those years ago.

She listened with growing dismay, searching her mother's face for reaction, finding there such a sober expression that her heart flipped. There was something wrong here, something very wrong.

Her uncle was explaining, 'We found these magnificent stones, very valuable they were, and plenty of them, but there was some mistake about our claim, an official's mistake, not ours...'

When he finished talking Danni pushed the jewel-case towards her mother but Lilyan shook her head.

'Put it away, Danni. We'll talk about it later.'

'All right. If you say so.' But Danni had to force herself to reach out and pick up the case.

A few minutes later her mother followed her to the caravan. She sat carefully on one of the beds, beckoning Danni to sit beside her.

'What made Jay North give you the brooch?'

Danni's soft mouth twisted ruefully. 'I told him his father stole it from us.'

Lilyan's sigh was deep and sad. 'I was afraid you might have.'

She handed Danni a faded letter. 'I'm afraid I'm a foolish parent. I keep overlooking that you're twenty-two years old and adult. We should have talked about this a few years ago,' her hands twisted nervously, 'but there didn't seem any need.

'Open it.' She nodded at the old letter. 'I should have talked to you about your uncle. I should have warned you. I'm afraid you—you can't always accept everything he says. He means well,' she added hastily, 'don't ever think he doesn't.'

'Of course not.' Danni glanced at the jewel-case on the bed between them. 'The brooch?' she prompted.

'Ah yes, the precious opal. I think it's time you read the letter. It's from your father, written to me when the boys abandoned their opal digging.'

Slowly, Danni unfolded the creased pages. Her father's writing, slanted, clear and carefully written, as if the writing was slow and painful.

> My darling wife,
>
> This is not the letter I planned to be writing to you today. All I can say is, I'm sorry. When we are together I will show you how grievously sorry I am.
>
> Our opal ventures have ended in disaster. Worse than disaster really, because we actually did find our pocket of stone and were filled with high hopes.
>
> I made arrangements for Edwin to carry our precious finds to a dealer in town, but he was apparently approached by a couple of out-of-town dealers who promised him the world, and you know Edwin, he fell for the old con. He was lured to an out-of-the-way location, attacked and robbed. So foolish. He should have been suspicious but they promised him the highest price, and he fell for it. I wanted to be angry but I couldn't, my darling. If you could have seen his poor, bruised face. He was quite devastated. There is no hope of the opals ever being re-

covered. Those rogues will be on the other side of Australia by now.

So we are coming home not rich but broke and disillusioned. Please don't be too angry with Edwin. I know you feel it's ridiculous that he has to be humoured and pampered but he means well.

I regret that I come back to you and our beloved children empty-handed and with less if possible than the little I brought here with me to Coober Pedy. Even the small opal I saved and made into a brooch for you will have to go—in some way a very small reparation to Gardiner North for the misfortune we have brought him. Only a drop in the bucket, I'm afraid, certainly not enough to save his family property, which is what brought him digging here with us. And we, my dear one, will have to start again.

I'm afraid I shall have to carry on taking care of Edwin, I hope it does not distress you too much, but I promised our parents.

He's a bungler, and I'm afraid with the best will in the world will bring always trouble for himself and those who work with him, yet I cannot let him flounder alone.

Forgive me, and I love you all,
    Your devoted,
    Ryan.

Danni put the letter down slowly. 'I can't understand how Uncle Edwin could tell all those lies. How can he say Gardiner North stole the brooch?'

'He believes it.' Lilyan's smile twisted. 'He believes everything he says, because he has to. He persuades himself that what he wants to be the truth actually is true. Otherwise he couldn't face himself, or us.' Lilyan picked up the faded letter and put it in her pocket. 'Your father explained it to me once. He said Edwin was the first child, born late in marriage, long after his parents had given up hope of having children. He was supposed to have some kind of heart-murmur, some weakness, and because of that frailty he was pampered. Later your father was born, and because their parents were wiser by that time, they took care to discipline your father. But Edwin never really grew up and faced reality.

'It was always Ryan's responsibility to care for Edwin, although he was the younger son, but he took it seriously. Too seriously, I often thought, because sometimes your father penalised himself in favour of his brother. Edwin never had to be accountable to anyone, not even to himself.'

'I wish you'd shown me the letter before.'

Lilyan sighed regretfully. 'I couldn't. I wanted to, but Edwin has taken care of us——'

Or you have taken care of Edwin, Danni thought, but she said, 'Of course,' and impulsively hugged her mother.

'Don't worry about it, Mums. But I think I'd better give the man back his jewellery, don't you?'

Her mother nodded. 'Yes. I'm sorry, Danni.'

'It doesn't matter. I don't want to keep it and I don't think you do either.'

After her mother left the caravan Danni sat staring at the jewel-case. The sensible thing to do was to put it with the typing for Jackson North to pick up when he called, but she didn't feel very sensible at the moment. She felt restless and impatient. And guilty. She wanted to give Jackson North his brooch as fast as she could get it to him.

When she heard footsteps approaching the caravan Danni made no attempt to move, because it was probably Gregg coming back with her notebook that she had left in the office, but when the door opened it was Derek's head and shoulders she saw. He didn't bother to knock, just pushed the door open wider and let himself in.

'Where the devil have you been?' he demanded crossly.

'You know where I've been,' Danni protested wearily.

'I'm not talking about the trip. You came back yesterday. Mother and I expected to see you last night. Gregg told Fiona you were back.'

'I was tired, and I had some work to do this morning.'

Derek's handsome face clouded. 'Mother made your favourite supper. Seafood and white wine; we had it waiting for you. We have a lot to talk over. The gallery has taken orders for more of your work.'

He was looking at her expectantly, waiting for her to be elated, and Danni wanted to scream. She felt a deep, deep urge to break into hysterical laughter. Why should she become ecstatic because Derek and his mother could sell a few painted shirts?

Then common sense and the desire to be fair to her friends came to Danni's rescue. She said warmly, 'That's really great. Thanks for telling me. I've made some sketches and roughed out a few ideas for more painted tops but I'll need a day or two to settle back home.'

He wasn't very pleased about that. 'Don't take too long. You'd best get busy while there's a demand. We can't guarantee how long any line will appeal to the public.'

He scrutinised her pale face, the shadows under her eyes, the faint droop of her shoulders.

'Did something happen I should hear about? You don't look too good.'

'Of course not. Nothing happened you should know about.'

He scrutinised her suspiciously, before his face lightened. 'We sold three paintings while you were away.'

Two or three weeks ago she would have hugged him with pleasure, now she braced herself, forcing enthusiasm.

'That's wonderful. Which ones?'

'Oh, just a couple of scenes of local beaches.' He sounded evasive and Danni understood why when he added with artificial casualness, 'And that one of the Glasshouse Mountains.'

He looked guilty. The Glasshouse Mountains painting was one Danni especially wanted. She was saving her money to buy it, and Derek knew that. The mountains with their granite cones thrust against the sky had always held special mystery and attention for Danni. She had really coveted that painting.

Derek muttered, 'Bloke made me an offer I couldn't refuse. Gallery-owner from Brisbane. Says he might get me more orders.'

He waited for Danni to tell him she didn't mind him selling the painting and she couldn't do it. As she studied the weak, handsome face she knew that would be the story of her life if she carried on her relationship with Fiona's brother.

She would be continually forgiving him for considering nobody but himself, excusing his self-interest, submerging herself and her own preferences to do what Derek wanted.

When she failed to reassure him he scowled. 'You're different,' he accused. 'What's happened?'

'I told you, I'm tired.' They both knew that wasn't all.

Derek insisted, 'Mother would like to see you now. We're having a special open day at the gallery on Sunday. We were relying on you.' He went on, 'We thought we might specialise in a display of souvenirs in the rear gallery while I set up an easel in the front so people can see me painting. It might boost sales.'

'I agree.'

'Then you'll come with me now and talk it over?'

'Not now.' Danni forced herself to counter Derek's hostile gaze. 'I told you, I've something to do.'

'Then you'd better buck up,' he advised her moodily. He scanned her pale features, her strained expression with the vividness somehow vanished, the sparkling personality muted, and what he saw obviously displeased him.

'You'd better call at the gallery when you're more like your real self again.'

He meant if she didn't sparkle she wouldn't attract sales, and suddenly Danni didn't really care. She said, 'I'm sorry, Derek. I really can't talk any more,' and he gaped at her incredulously.

He had always been the one to break off an encounter, calling the tune as to how they met and where.

He said, 'You certainly must be in a hurry to do whatever it is,' and she told him, 'Yes, I am.'

He stared at her, offended. There was a hardness in his pale blue eyes she hadn't seen before, as he realised she was not as biddable as she had been before.

'You've always been reliable.' He meant she had always done what he told her to do. Danni hadn't known it, but she had spent the last couple of years being manipulated. Now she looked at Derek, sizing him up, seeing him clearly for the first time.

Derek didn't like being thwarted. He scowled. 'Mother and I need your help, I might remind you,' and when Danni didn't answer he added snappily, 'I suppose we could easily get somebody else.'

That was his exit line. He banged the caravan door after him, and Danni flinched, but as she listened to his retreating footsteps she became aware that instead of being stricken, as Derek so obviously hoped, she had in her heart the most wonderful and blessed feeling of release.

CHAPTER TEN

DANNI moved swiftly. She felt motivated, as if she had received a charge of energy. She took the first swimsuit she found in her wardrobe—a red and white spotted maillot—put it on and covered it with white shorts. In her wardrobe she found a blue waterproof jacket she had borrowed one day from Gregg and forgotten to give back. She put it on, folded the jewel-case in a plastic bag and tucked it into one pocket, buttoning the flap carefully.

She smeared her limbs and face quickly with suncream, tied her hair back with a white scarf, and now she was ready.

She knew exactly what she was doing. She was setting her sail for the island where Jay most likely sat poring over his notes in the headland cabin.

If Eleanor was there with him then she, Danni, was headed straight for humiliation.

'I must be crazy,' she told herself light-headedly as she stepped out of the caravan.

Gregg was mowing grass along the verge of the driveway. He grinned when he saw her wearing his jacket.

'I charge rental.'

'I'm going out to the island,' Danni told him. 'Can you take care of reception?'

'Of course I can, sister dear. You are not indispensable.'

He didn't ask which island. He didn't have to. One glimpse of the resolution in her face told him exactly where she was heading. He gave an impish grin and Danni said, 'If I'm not back tonight, don't worry.'

'Like that, is it? Well, give him my regards. Hope you get a welcome.' But he wasn't trying to put her off, just teasing. If anything, he looked pleased she was heading Jackson North's way.

Danni got into the little red car and drove along the riverside to the ocean beach. Her sailboard was in the boatshed and she dragged it out, carrying board and sail to the water's edge.

Somebody called her name. It was Fiona, and Danni waved and called, 'Hi!'

Fiona came running, her face anxious. 'Danni, are you all right?'

'Of course.' White lie. Danni was not sure she would be all right.

'Derek's upset. He's worried about you.'

'I know. I'm sorry.'

Fiona wanted to say more but Danni couldn't stay. Right at this moment she dared not stop for anyone.

She was going to Jay, and she could be headed for the biggest put-down of her life, but whatever waited for her out on that blue smudge of island, it was better than suspense.

If she was going to be unceremoniously dumped, brushed off for Eleanor, then she would find out now. Not tomorrow.

The wind in her sail was strong and invigorating, blowing tension away. Danni felt the adrenalin flow as she manoeuvred, bracing herself with legs astride and using her body to contest the vagaries of the strong breeze. She had missed the sea. The ballooning coloured sail was magic.

She set her course for Jay's island, and the emotions that were taking life and shape in her mind were as colourful as the sail. She knew where they sprang from, they had everything to do with that one fantastic night under the stars when she and Jay had made love; and somewhere deep in her body, even as she bent and thrust herself against the pull of the wind in her sail, an undeniable need stirred and stayed.

She must see Jay. She had made an unforgivable mistake, when she accused him of being her family's enemy, so she would not ask him to forgive her, but she couldn't ride fast enough to return his beautiful opal bird. With apologies, she reminded herself. Oh yes, there would have to be apologies.

As she neared the island she remembered the empty shell of the house that had once been Jay's family home. Very different from the small cabin on the headland. No wonder he was angry, although he was the achiever now, the high-flyer, rich and successful beyond his father's dreams.

She reached the coral reef and found the entrance, beaching her board on the white sand. Jay was not watching her approach this time. She would have known, she was sure.

She dragged the sailboard to the top of the sand and began walking, and there was no tingling of her skin, no prickling awareness. She could have been alone on the island.

The blue jacket flapped in the breeze and the shorts clung wetly to her hips. She could have shaken her hair loose to dry as she walked, but something stopped her, and she walked the whole long beach without looking back, impelled by will-power, knowing in her heart that if she paused to think she might easily turn back, even now, and that would be a disaster.

She kept recalling Jay's bitter face as he looked into the ruined homestead, the savage way he had broken off that solitary flower.

Jay had been hurt deeply, and if she and her family had played a part in that hurt then it was up to her to risk a little damage to her own pride if she could set some part of the record straight. Because she knew now that what she felt for Jay was not only the lighting of physical fires, the surge of passion. It was tenderness. Tenderness and caring. A need to see him, even if he felt for her only bitterness and contempt.

Danni would not allow herself to look further than the prospect of a blow to her ego. A little humiliation couldn't hurt anybody.

But of course that was a lie. She could be walking towards the deepest hurt of her young life; but she owed Jay and she intended to pay the debt.

She reached the end of the beach and climbed the track leading up to Jay's retreat. She murmured to herself, 'Lionel should be here,' but of course the small dog could be frisking anywhere on the island.

He hadn't been around on her last visit. There must be countless fascinating temptations to keep a curious dog busy on an island like this.

The door of Jackson North's cabin stood half-open. Danni rapped on it twice before his voice called tersely, 'All right. Come in.'

Did that mean he knew who she was? Or was he expecting Eleanor?

Danni pushed one hand into the jacket pocket, fingering the jewel-case.

'I'm coming.'

So now he knew it was her. Not Eleanor. Not some total stranger.

Danni walked carefully across the living-room and found Jay as she had expected, sitting at the desk in his study with his notes strewn around him.

She hadn't noticed until then the small trickles of water shed by the jacket and shorts, collecting around her feet.

Jay looked pointedly at the drops trickling on to his carpet and Danni said in confusion, 'I'm sorry. I didn't realise I was still wet. I'll take off my jacket.'

She hurried back to the veranda, hanging the jacket over a railing, collecting the jewel-case out of the pocket, holding it out to Jay as she came back into the study.

'I've brought you this,' she said inanely. 'Seems it belongs to you.'

He flicked her with a cool glance.

'What brought this on?'

She dropped it on to the desk, and pushed it closer to his hand.

'My mother showed me a letter my father wrote to her years ago, explaining why he gave the opals to your father. So it's yours, isn't it? I'm sorry.'

Jay put down his pen. He didn't seem at all interested in the jewellery. He was looking at her, very quietly, just looking, and it seemed to Danni then that what she saw in his eyes was not only strength and power and dominance but also a suggestion of vulnerability. He always seemed so sure of himself. Now the grey eyes could have held a question, as if he were waiting for something.

She waited breathlessly until he said,

'Is that all you've brought me?'

'You mean the script? You're waiting for it?'

'No, I don't mean the script. I was thinking of something more personal.'

Hope leaped in Danni then but Jay's expression remained inscrutable. She must not let herself get carried away.

She said carefully, 'What else were you expecting?'

He didn't answer, but he pushed his chair back and stood up, and then he disappeared into the next room just as he had done on the day of her first visit to the island. Again, he returned with a white shirt over his arm.

'History repeats itself.' His lips twisted. 'For heaven's sake, put that on. That's a mighty enticing body you have there, Danielle. I don't mind telling you my self-control is slipping. So cover yourself, if you don't mind.'

Danni made no move to put on the shirt. Jay settled himself in the chair, watching her, saying nothing, and Danni mumbled, 'Where's Lionel?'

'I don't know. Don't tell me you came out here to see Lionel. He's off chasing possums or lizards. How should I know?'

There would be no end to the pain in her heart until she asked her next question.

'And Eleanor? Where is she?'

Jay frowned, his expression blank, and when he said nothing Danni confessed, 'You talked about her when you got that bump on the head. You kept saying her name. Eleanor. Who is she?'

Jay frowned at the desk, then suddenly his face cleared.

'Lord! Is that what went wrong?'

He pushed the typewriter away from him and stood up again, glaring at her across the desk-top.

'I should break you in half, Danni Paige. Do you have any idea what you put me through?'

'Eleanor——?'

Danni pressed her lips together to stop them quivering, and he came around to her side of the desk, standing close, running his palms over her shoulders, down her arms, bending to kiss her softly.

'If you want to see Eleanor you'll have to come into the other room with me.'

He pointed to the bedroom and Danni drew sharply away from him, but Jay's face was tender.

'Come with me.' He coaxed her into the room. As Danni expected this was his bedroom, built-in wardrobes along two walls, a double bed under the window, and beside the bed a small table with a bedlamp. No photographs. Nothing that could be Eleanor.

Jay watched half smiling as Danni searched the room with her eyes, looking for Eleanor, finding nobody. Then he guided her to the window, pulled back the curtains and pointed to the peaks of the two hills in the middle of the island.

'You mean, Eleanor lives up there?'

He laughed. 'Not Eleanor. Illunah. Those two hills are Illunah and Benjaree, the central characters in an Aboriginal legend. Would you like to hear it?'

Danni nodded, stunned. So there was no Eleanor... The love and tenderness in his face on that dreadful night had not been for somebody else.

Jay was telling her gently, 'It is said that in the Dreamtime, thousands of years ago, a young mainland warrior named Benjaree offended his totem spirit, the Emu, by casting covetous eyes on a maiden from a forbidden tribe. So he was taken by the Emu to the great Rainbow Serpent for judgement, and condemned to live in exile on this island for the rest of his life, to keep him out of trouble.

'After a few years he became so lonely and miserable the Rainbow Serpent felt sorry for him, so he was allowed a few visits from Illunah, one of the sea-maidens who takes care of life in the ocean.

'Benjaree fathered three children from Illunah, and after the birth of each child the sea-maiden had to leave her lover and go back to the sea to fulfil her duties and look after the sea creatures that were in her care.'

Jay told the story in a gentle voice, as if it were something special to him, and Danni listened enchanted.

'Poor Benjaree. What did he do while she was gone?'

'Not very much, apparently. He spent a lot of time moping. He fished and did a little hunting, finding lizards in the sand and possums in the trees, and he took care of his children. But most of the time he sat on the shore and sang sad songs, waiting for his sea-maiden to return, until after her fourth visit his need of her was so great he managed to persuade Illunah to stay with him.

'They hid in a cave on the other side of the island and for a while they avoided the avenging spirits.

'But of course eventually they were found, and the angry Rainbow Serpent changed them into those two big hills. The foothills are their four children. So now they live here for ever. Or at least,' Jay amended whimsically, 'until erosion or storms wear them away.'

'I think that's a very sad story.' But Danni's heart was singing.

Jay smiled at her indulgently. 'Not really. When tribal people wandered freely on the mainland they always refused to come out to this island in bad weather, because the legend says that whenever the hilltops are shrouded in rain or sea-mist, Benjaree and Illunah are allowed to become themselves again and make love for just as long as the mist hides them. Which is sometimes,' the grey eyes glinted at her, 'in very bad weather, a very long time indeed. Could be days.'

Jay was smiling at her, his mouth made a tantalising curve, and Danni said demurely, 'What a dire punishment! Fancy having to make love for days.'

'Shouldn't be too difficult for a man in love. Shall I prove it to you, Danni?'

Suddenly he was serious, taking her in his arms, telling her, 'Danni, if you hadn't come out here today I would have come after you. I knew I couldn't last another night.' His hand cradled her head against him. 'Illunah, my sea-maiden. I had a feeling about you that day when you first came out here, and I watched you and your bright sail coming over the water. I was using binoculars and I had this premonition that something—something—well—predestined, was about to happen to me.

I tried to shake it off, but my intuition was going flat out, disturbing me. And when I saw it was you—my critic from the studio——'

'You remembered.' Danni pulled a small ashamed face. 'I hoped you'd forgotten, then when you mentioned television studios I knew I was in for it.'

He traced the shape of her lips with one potent fingertip. 'There was little chance of my forgetting.' His voice became reflective.

'I saw you step out of the lift and I told myself, that's one hell of a lady, and I hung around most of the morning after the interview was done, hoping to bump into you again. I went to the canteen for lunch hoping to find you. I was trying to invent a plausible excuse for breaking into your conversation with those other two girls when you made your—er—unfortunate remark.'

He teased her, 'You certainly dropped the bucket on me,' and Danni apologised ruefully,

'I'm sorry. It was a silly thing to say, and I shouldn't have spoken loudly enough for you to hear. But I honestly didn't know you were there.'

'That's all right. I could see why you got the impression I was attention-grabbing, though I was mad as hell to hear you say it. We needed all the promotion we could get. If signing autographs could persuade a few more viewers to watch the documentaries, all the better. Little did I know,' he ran sensuous fingers through her hair, untying the knotted scarf deftly, 'little did I know I was going to earn the disapproval of the most intriguing young woman I'd ever seen.'

'Am I intriguing?' Danni widened her green eyes innocently. 'You haven't shown much sign of noticing it lately.'

'Is that why you didn't cover yourself with that shirt I brought in for you?'

'No.' Danni gazed up at him, clear-eyed. 'To be honest I——' She searched his face for the loving tenderness she hoped to find there. When she was almost certain she found it, she went on bravely, 'I was hoping you'd find me more than intriguing. Irresistible, I guess, among other things. And that you would——' Despite her resolution a faint flush crept into Danni's cheeks. It wasn't every day a girl abandoned pride, leaving herself open to the great snub in her life. 'That you would——'

'Yes?' Jay said huskily, bending to kiss her forehead with light, warm lips. 'That I would make love to you?'

'That's right.'

So now he knew. She had thrown herself at him without reserve. Quietly, Danni awaited his reaction. She thought she knew how he felt, but how could she be certain, especially when it mattered so much?

Jay cupped her face in his hands, teasing laughter in his voice.

'I could be persuaded to make love to you,' he offered.

'Isn't that your prerogative?'

'After an invitation like that,' he slid his fingers under the narrow straps of her swimsuit, easing them down from her shoulders before he coaxed her gently on to the bed, 'how could I refuse?'

He stood for a few minutes looking down at her, a muscle flexing on his jawline, suddenly serious.

'The past two days have been very long,' he admitted soberly. 'I didn't know what happened to change your mind after that night in the desert, whether you thought I'd taken advantage of you, or decided I wasn't what you wanted, but whatever it was, I knew I was going to do whatever I could to put everything back in place after I'd given you time to settle down. The truth is, I don't think I can live without you, Danielle. I've convinced myself about that, even if I have yet to persuade you.'

He was pulling off his shirt, loosening the belt of his jeans as he gazed down at her, waiting for her to beckon him, to tell him she could be persuaded.

Danni spread out her arms, arching her body in a provocative curve.

'How many days did you say Illunah and her lover can make love in the mist?'

'Let's make it one or two to start with.' Free of his clothes, he stepped across and pulled the curtains over the window.

'Let's not be brazen about it,' he added cheerfully. 'We can't have the possums looking in.'

'I thought possums were nocturnal. Shouldn't they all be asleep?'

Jay bent to slowly, erotically, peel the scanty swimsuit from Danni's unresisting body.

'You never can tell with possums. There could be an occasional non-conformer.'

He settled himself beside her, and that was the last light-hearted comment that he made.

The arms he held out to her were hungry arms, trembling with need and expectation, and Danni rolled over to shape her naked body close to his, not one shred of doubt or resistance in her, only a swelling of feelings, emotions and passions from somewhere deep in her heart.

She was his for the taking and she let him know it, pulling him closer to her, moulding her hips to his, and he made a stifled sound deep in his throat before he laughed, almost triumphantly, like a young boy launching on his first love affair.

'Danni, you bring me the world. Everything wonderful, everything I'll ever need. I'll never let you go.'

She told him then, about the way he looked, about it being his first love affair, and a thousand amusements danced in his eyes.

'Not the first, regrettably, but definitely the last. The last and the greatest.'

He touched her throat with his lips, sliding his hands around her waist, igniting wild sensation, setting a thousand fires leaping, laughing exultantly as Danni moved under his touch.

He held her a little away from him, as though he were teasing himself.

'I promise you, I never had an experience that could touch that night we spent in the desert.'

Then again he gathered her towards him, pressing her against his body so that Danni felt enveloped in the heat and desire that fired him.

Her arms curved around his neck, pulling his head down so that their breaths mingled before their lips touched, and then once again an explosion of sensation lifted them out of this world and away into an environment where there was nothing but wave after wave of pleasure experienced at unbelievable intensity.

And when it was over Danni lay beside her lover, emotional and yet somehow clear-thinking, exhausted yet uplifted, and totally satisfied.

She felt Jay's fingers curling tightly around her hand, and she reached up with her free arm and dreamily touched his face. He kissed her lightly.

'Some day after we're married, some day soon,' he murmured softly, 'I'll take you up to the top of the hill and we will make love there, and make our peace with Benjaree and Illunah. I feel we owe it to them.'

'Yes.' Danni lifted the hand that held hers to her lips. 'That should entertain the possums.' Her voice bubbled with laughter and happiness, and he laughed back at her, then pulled her quickly towards him.

'Forget the possums,' he told her huskily, tracing the rise and fall of her breasts with one fingertip, bending to tease and kiss the trail of sensation he aroused. 'Come and make more love with me, my maiden from the sea.'

Although he said it lightly, lifting his head to smile beguilingly at her, Danni knew that it was a promise and a commitment.

She offered him her body for his pleasure and her own, and this time he took it gently, as if he understood that with it came her heart and all her love and caring, everything that she had ever been or ever would be.

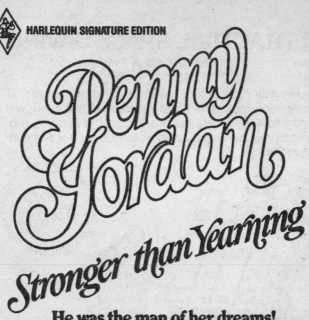

Penny Jordan

Stronger than Yearning

He was the man of her dreams!

The same dark hair, the same mocking eyes; it was as if the Regency rake of the portrait, the seducer of Jenna's dream, had come to life. Jenna, believing the last of the Deverils dead, was determined to buy the great old Yorkshire Hall—to claim it for her daughter, Lucy, and put to rest some of the painful memories of Lucy's birth. She had no way of knowing that a direct descendant of the black sheep Deveril even existed—or that James Allingham and his own powerful yearnings would disrupt her plan entirely.

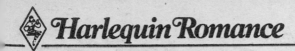
Coming Next Month

2911 FLIRTATION RIVER Bethany Campbell
When the daughter of a U.S. senator is sent into hiding after
receiving a series of anonymous letters threatening her life,
her handsome protector provides not only safety, but a kind
of happiness she'd never known before.

2912 RECIPE FOR LOVE Kay Clifford
Vicky is stunned when the J. P. Duncan who registered for a
place in her women's summer cookery course turns out to
be a man. She soon discovers that Jay has more than cookery
on his mind!

2913 CLOUDED PARADISE Rachel Ford
Unless Catherine can get rid of the squatter living on her
beach property, she can't sell it. But Luke Devenish is
determined to stay and makes it clear that he despises rich
heiresses like Catherine.

2914 A GENTLE AWAKENING Betty Neels
Florina loves her new job as cook in the home of consultant
Sir William Sedley, and before long she realizes she loves Sir
William, too! Unfortunately Sir William is already engaged
to the glamorous but entirely unsuitable Wanda.

2915 CAPTURE A NIGHTINGALE Sue Peters
Ros doesn't really mind going to Majorca to help out the
eccentric painter Mildred Fisher. But when disaster
threatens her journey, she can't help wondering how safe
she'll be in the hands of overbearing Keel Hennessy, her
traveling companion.

2916 UNFRIENDLY ALLIANCE Jessica Steele
When Anstey is literally left holding her friend's baby, she
turns for help to the child's uncle, the powerful, forbidding
Cale Quartermaine. She isn't prepared, however, to have
Cale rearrange her life as well as the baby's!

Available in June wherever paperback books are sold, or
through Harlequin Reader Service:

In the U.S.
901 Fuhrmann Blvd.
P.O. Box 1397
Buffalo, N.Y. 14240-1397

In Canada
P.O. Box 603
Fort Erie, Ontario
L2A 5X3